# THE
# BEHOLDER

# THE
# BEHOLDER

*a novel*

## THOMAS FARBER

METROPOLITAN BOOKS

Henry Holt and Company | New York

Metropolitan Books
Henry Holt and Company, LLC
*Publishers since 1866*
115 West 18th Street
New York, New York 10011

Metropolitan Books™ is a registered
trademark of Henry Holt and Company, LLC.

Published in Canada by Fitzhenry & Whiteside Ltd.,
195 Allstate Parkway, Markham, Ontario L3R 4T8.

Library of Congress Cataloging-in-Publication Data

Farber, Thomas, 1944–
    The beholder : a novel / by Thomas Farber.— 1st. ed.
        p.    cm.
    ISBN 0-8050-6972-0 (hc.)
    I. Title.
PS3556.A64 B44 2002
813'.54—dc21                    2001055781

    Henry Holt books are available for special
promotions and premiums. For details contact:
        Director, Special Markets.

First Edition 2002

*Designed by Paula Russell Szafranski*

Printed in the United States of America

1   3   5   7   9   10   8   6   4   2

*For Niki*

To our bodies turn we then, that so

    Weak men on love reveal'd may look;

Love's mysteries in souls do grow,

    But yet the body is his book.

              John Donne, "The Exstasie"

# THE
# BEHOLDER

# REPRESENTATIONS

Once upon a time ... her aunt phones. A friend of friends, émigré nobility living in California some ten years, the aunt takes a while to get to the point. Politesse; palace intrigue. Gist of her circumlocutions: precocious niece finishing Ph.D. in art history, already teaching at a local college. Also trying fiction. Can he meet with the niece?

To read a manuscript, pass on names of editors or agents, or occasionally to mentor: part of a writer's life. So, coffee with, as it turns out, a lovely young woman. Who then invites him to a party she and her husband are giving. Saying he regrets he can't make it, the writer suggests lunch. They talk novels, movies, painters. She's finishing Schama on Rembrandt; he recites a Larkin poem; she's brought some Rilke. He gives her one of his own books, says she can keep it if she likes. She recounts the stormy life of Caravaggio.

Thus they meet, twice, and she's married, has what seems to him a loud diamond ring. Perhaps, he decides, because her charm and wit are so flirtatious. High heels, makeup, large blue eyes, lips very red. Dressy, for academia. Theatrical.

The writer likes seeing her. Hardworking, ambitious. Self-absorbed, but why not? A perquisite of beauty. Drinking in concerts, lectures. And, she says, her husband spoils her. Vain, a bit of a coquette (the word's just about archaic, he thinks).

Also, she has an air of being young for her age, a kind of adolescent hunger for absolutes. Fervor about, say, the Meaning of Art. Once, she asks the writer to explain why Art matters.

"Tell you the truth, I just try to do my books." Deflecting the question: he's spent his adult life at his métier, has had to consider its qualities.

"I know it must sound foolish." Laughs at her own expense. Finding such self-deprecation winning, he wonders if this is the kind of concern he had in his early twenties.

In any case, she's married, but has yet to tell her aunt. Old story: authority figure objects to beloved, youth ducks the battle. So, "kind of a secret." Shared with the writer after he explains that his late mother never saw her mother again once she married. But this young woman does see her aunt, simply hasn't mentioned that her life has changed.

This particular afternoon, she visits the writer's cottage for the first time. He'd avoided inviting her, prefers meeting people out in the world, both to control the pace and, sometimes, requiring a provocation to leave his study. But now he's said she might want to see "a writer's habitat."

They're in the living room. The writer sits across from her on the love seat in the alcove. It's hard for him to make out some of her words because of her soft voice and slight accent—she arrived in the United States at seventeen.

"Why don't you come over here?" The sentence sounds abrupt. The writer thinks he can hear her weigh it.

"All right." She gets up, crosses the room, sits beside him.

Later, he suggests that she check out the cottage if she likes.

"Where do you sleep?" she asks, after looking into the two bedrooms.

"Depends who else is here." Immediately, seeing her expression, revises. "Downstairs. Upstairs when I have houseguests."

"Oh."

She continues to wander. He remembers his friend Fred telling him the young have no content, are all ideas. And ruthless. She's in his cottage, examining it, him. A kind of collector. Not much more, though she later says all such encounters carry sexual ambiguity. Still, knowledge is what she's after. He's source material.

So, she's in the attic, years ago converted to a library. Sections of books on Hawai'i, ocean, surfing, Pacific Island literature. Not of much interest to her. Descending the stairs to the study, she sits on a step reading titles on the facing shelves. Above the books on death and lying are sex and/or the erotic. *The Female Nude,* by Lynda Nead; Janet Hobhouse's *The Bride Stripped Bare.* "Mmmm," she says, as if tasting a sweet. "I like these." Picks up yet another book, slips it back in place. Seeing this, he feels a sense of kinship. She's doing what he'd do, has done so many times. If years before, when he was her age, you asked him to choose between the woman in front of him or her bookcases, well, he'd have contrived to take in both. Would have asked for pencil and paper.

"Do you want pencil and paper?"

"No thank you." Still browsing.

Kinship; she is oddly like . . . not oneself, but oneself were he a young woman. Not a sentiment he remembers experiencing.

"I'd love to work my way through these shelves," she says. "I treasure books, perhaps too much." She hesitates. "A long time ago, someone I cared for told me, 'Life's not a book.'"

"Too true," he replies, mulling the "cared for."

As for the titles she's been looking at, she knows he's interested in academic discourse on the female figure. That first day at coffee, he'd mentioned Balzac's *Unknown Masterpiece,* famous tale depicting three artists and a model.

6

Subsequently, at lunch, she brought a book about the Balzac to loan him. Thus, he's not surprised when she asks, "I don't quite understand what you're exploring in this area."

Fair question, but his answer startles him.

"It's related to working with figure models."

*"Figure models?"*

He can't believe it. As with all work in progress, he's kept it to himself. So many empowering privacies. "You know, having them pose."

"In art class?"

"No. Right here in the study. Like Rodin in his sixties. The models he kept around his atelier, the thousands of sketches."

"I've written about Rodin in my thesis."

"Well, I'm younger than Rodin was"—he chides himself for this—"and less obsessed. I think." He pauses, trying to slow down.

"So how do you do it?"

"Just what I'd want to know. I bring a chair from the living room, the model sits over there, near the desk. I'm not sure where it's going. Part of being a writer is being able to wait to find out."

She smiles. "You said models, plural. How many, if you don't mind my asking."

"I don't mind." Still feeling he's making a mistake. "Maybe twenty the last two years. I have some models return. But no photographs, no sketching. Also, just one at a time."

"But no photographs, no sketching? What are you doing?"

"Oh, I suppose I thought, why should only visual artists get to study the female form? But also, I felt I'd never looked carefully enough at women. Too much pursuit, need. What had I failed to see?"

She nods. He'd not articulated this before, has, as usual, just launched himself into another three- or five-year book mania.

"How do you do it?"

"They sit in the chair, on a towel—a clean towel."

"Such generosity!"

"Please. You asked. So, same chair, same place. Constraint of form, like rhyme or meter. They take off their clothes in the bathroom, walk in here. I'm at the desk, computer on. I've already explained how it will work when they call to answer the ad."

"Ad?"

"'Author seeks figure model, female,' and so on."

"Did you get many responses?"

"Forty, fifty. Some women called over and again."

"God, you are crazy." He hears the admiration.

"Yes. Anyway, I tell the model we can talk or not talk. Some take a book off the shelf, read. A book I've written, perhaps. If they do talk, I try to catch a sense of how they speak. Meanwhile I'm looking, and sketching them in words on the computer. It's a lot of work, actually."

"I'll bet."

"Really. Then I make notes after they leave. One model

a day is more than plenty. One a week. It's been months since the last session. I'm trying to figure out where I'm going." Suddenly he feels exhausted.

"Are you going to make notes after I leave?"

He maneuvers to gather himself. "You haven't modeled," he responds, and they both laugh.

Manet's *Olympia*, first shown in Paris in 1865, provoked shock, hostility. No mythological maiden, but a young working-class woman from Paris. Invisible Renaissance nipples, no pubic hair, self-caressing hand on thigh summoning the observer's attention. The writer studies the painting, reads conflicting critical opinions about it. Not, he thinks, that anyone can talk about *Olympia* without implicating himself. Herself.

Olympia-the-model, Victorine Meurent, in her late teens, had already posed for other artists, eventually became a painter. And why Victorine for Manet? Her flair for mimicry? Because she was simply a mannequin? Whatever: Manet painted Victorine in various guises—as "herself"; as matador; as street singer; without clothes.

Meanwhile, *Olympia*'s famous gaze. Defiant? Indifferent? During the young woman's visit to the cottage, they discussed the painting. At one point, fixing her eyes on the writer, she formed a half-circle at her throat with thumb and forefinger: Olympia's ribbon.

"Isn't the question on most minds," she then said, very pleased with herself, "whether or not Olympia's looking at a man she knows well? And, if so, how well?"

They're leaving the cottage that day.

"Your heroic enterprise with the models makes me think of Dürer," she says. "*Draftsman Drawing a Nude.* The artist at his worktable, paper blocked out, his bulging eyes devouring the reclining woman. It's amusing: she's on the far side of that gridded screen—well out of reach. Her lower body is draped. There's all the technology of art, and so much not happening."

"You're comparing me to the draftsman?"

She laughs. Standing beside her at the front gate, the writer feels he's made a mistake giving up that privacy of his.

As if sensing his dismay, she asks, "May I describe your project to my husband?" Reminding him, he supposes, that she's very married.

"Do what you want," he replies, more curtly than he intended. And, compounding the error, "You're a grown-up."

"What do you prefer?" No defensiveness.

What does he prefer? Why's that important? And compared to what else that's important?

She's waiting.

"I prefer you tell anyone else I'm doing research on representations of the female figure in Western art."

"All right. No problem."

"No problem": her colloquial English is rich with the savor of irony. And, the writer realizes, she's consented to several things at once.

A week later, he receives a letter.

> I've been thinking about your intriguingly transgressive project. Art historians say that nothing is more difficult to render than flesh. I especially appreciate that you don't yet know where you are going. I'd also suppose, given your writing, that you're not going to try to compete with visual artists. Leonardo, in the *Paragone,* wrote that it would be hopeless to try to do in words what a painter does in a moment. Perhaps the simultaneous movement of so many compelling aspects—hands, lips, eyes—is just too nuanced and quicksilver for the verbal. Or perhaps you'll prove the contrary.
>
> Either way, I fear that in all the banter I failed to make this clear: I'm very glad we met.

Rereading the letter, the writer mutters "transgressive, quicksilver." Sees that the return address is her aunt's home.

.  .  .

The writer has a banker friend, just divorced, very lonely. "A fringe benefit of art," he tells the writer, "is that women admire artists."

"Well," the writer replies, hearing the unstated "you have it easy," "if you're changing vocations, to spend so much time in one's study can hardly be the shortest path to eros. Try teaching tango."

But of course the writer could argue it differently. Knows an older author, still publishing, who likes to insist his earlier fiction was peacock feather–spreading. Pure mating behavior.

Now this young woman, her apparent idealization, despite teasing, of the risks she imagines the writer's taken. They meet again, after about a month. Quick coffee; she's on her way to teach. She seems preoccupied, and the writer's uncomfortable: what are they doing anyway?

He walks her to the BART train. A glorious northern California day: high, blue, clear, recent rains having left everything sparkling. Plum and cherry starting to bloom.

They're moving fast—she's late. He's carrying her satchel. "God, this is heavy."

"I told you I like books. Are you impressed?"

"Sobered."

"Good."

As they reach the station, he says, "You know, we're

lucky to be alive for such a lovely day." She looks at him almost quizzically, he thinks. "I'm glad we could share a bit of it," he adds.

"Me too," she responds. Takes the satchel, disappears down the stairs.

Leafing through his notes, the writer comes across a description of the male artist in Shaw's *Man and Superman:* "half vivisector, half vampire," using women "to surprise their inmost secrets . . . to make him see visions and dream dreams, to inspire him, as he calls it." Which puts the writer in mind of a serial rapist who, years before, terrorized his neighborhood. Finally apprehended, the rapist proved to be an amateur photographer, deft at asking a stranger if he could take her picture, offering prints in return. Many women—none of them his rape victims—undressed in exchange for the art rendered.

Visions. Dreams. How one beholds the object of desire. And/or, "the gaze" of seducer, seduced. Who's curious, who's subjugated, who identifies with whom, how? To some thinkers, seeing is metamorphosis for seer and seen, bound to the disorder and cruelties of sex. Others argue that men make a fetish of women, denying the female body meaning of its own.

In his *Confessions,* Rousseau recounts how, at thirty, he's in Venice. No Casanova, Rousseau's been alone in a party town, having a "disgust for prostitutes," other women unavailable. One day, he's approached by a young courtesan. A whirlwind, she pretends to mistake him for someone else, theatrically claims possession. When they next meet, Rousseau's in a state of rapture. About to have such "sweet pleasure" bestowed on him, however, Rousseau begins to wonder, Why me? Of course, Rousseau cannot *not* work it out: "I perceived that she had a malformed nipple. . . ." Now Rousseau held in his arms a "Monster, rejected by Nature, men, and love." Not surprisingly, she tells him, *"Lascia le donne, e studia la matematica."* Give up the ladies, and study mathematics.

The writer ponders Rousseau's story. How often, he thinks, has he studied his own kind of mathematics?

The models. One gets to stare. What about it? Stimulation through gazing, or exposing oneself to the gaze of another, is for psychoanalysts a twisted form of penetrating the other. In this scheme of things, there can be active and sadistic desire to gaze, or passive, masochistic desire to be gazed at. From which, it's argued, emerge curiosity and artistic display.

Writer, ruminating. No one stands outside the conversation, he thinks. Each story partial, each narrator blind to or suppressing aspects of character, history. What about the exuberance of looking? Visual feasting? The writer laughs. Gloomy, these analysts. As if they believe we're all just too much for ourselves. Deep waters indeed. But, he's sure, nothing from which to avert one's eyes.

As for the writer's current effort to see things for what they are, so to speak, this compelling young woman commended the daybooks and photographs of Edward Weston. Now he has a new stack of titles beside his desk. Weston's female nudes, hundreds of them, face often omitted. Geometry—of breast, torso, thigh, back; narrative erased. Charis Wilson, one of Weston's wives and models, wrote that Weston took his pictures of her before making love. Almost dancing with his three-legged camera, carrying the model beyond exhibitionism or narcissism.

In his daybooks, Weston, then around forty, asked, "Why this tide of women?"

This tide of women. Large and small, older and younger, more or less beautiful to the writer—he accepts the models who most want the job. Reading that Greek friends of Weston told him there were three perfect shapes—hull of boat, violin, and a woman's body—the writer's tempted to demur. To counter with, say, waves, chambered nautilus, the branching patterns of trees. Nonetheless, surfer and sailor, guitarist, and now staring, very hard, at the models, he concludes that the proposition surely bears looking into.

Not long after the day they have coffee, he gives a reading at a nearby bookstore. In the audience are neighbors, a former lover, and friends who've known him as a writer nearly three decades. Waiting to be introduced, he sees her sit down in the back.

Afterward, people come up to chat. She stays in her seat, wearing a Discman, reading. Finally, crowd thinning, she approaches the lectern. He beckons, introduces her to several people.

"A glass of wine next door in a few minutes?" he asks.

She nods. "No hurry."

What's different, he wonders, facing her. First time he's seen her at night. And it's unusually warm, like the summer evenings of his high school and college years in Boston, green, leafy, humid, slow. He's wired, still, from the reading.

"Shouldn't you be with friends?" she asks.

"It's fine: they know I can be antisocial." He laughs. "Tell me, what were you listening to?"

"Lieder. Are you familiar with them?"

"Oh, yes. My mother was an accomplished soprano, had a concert career. Schubert and Schumann were part of childhood. Lyrics with all kinds of leave-takings, sorrows."

"How lucky you were. Such ethereal songs make my heart tremble, make me long to be a better person, for a story with grand closure."

The writer refrains from explaining how he resisted lieder as an adolescent. Too much high culture, too consonant with Puritan graveyards, the relentless limits of winter. After he first saw northern California at twenty, he returned to stay, rock and roll on the car radio. No death in California, he thought.

As if having decided something, she says, "My American friends think because I've been with just one man that

I'm repressed." She pauses. "I have a great passion for the person I love. It's not repression, but renunciation. That's quite different."

"I'm sure it is." And, feeling another affirmative's required, "Yes."

She looks at her watch. As if by mutual assent, they prepare to leave. At the door, they embrace. Pull back, look at each other carefully.

"Good night," she says. "It was wonderful to see you."

"Same here. See you again soon, I hope."

Several days after the reading, the writer leaves for Hawai'i, for many years one of his compass points, homes. Always the *moana*—the ocean. Saved by (warm) water. This trip, however, is to research an essay about an abandoned sugar mill and banyan grove he'd stumbled on years before.

The tropics: stupefied in the midday heat, writer in the cane fields wandering dirt roads. Finally spotting a dome of dense foliage, and, through the canopy, a man-made structure. Slipping down a row of cane, entering the shell of a decrepit building. The writer has a photograph of this agricultural factory in its nineteenth-century prime: smoke-stack, migrant laborers, ox-drawn carts. But now, dissolution, collapse. And banyans. Melded branches and trunks like a pipe fitter's mania, superglued to walls. Walls smothered, strangled. Sunlight remote beyond the leaf umbrella; no visual escape. The breeze picks up, sound of a plane far off accentuating the isolation. Goose bumps: chicken skin, as they put it in Hawai'i. Out of the mill, quick, into the blinding light, down that orderly row of cane. Large sky above. Ocean green/jade-blue/violet.

Before departing, the writer had described his project.

"Do you know about the bodhi tree?" she'd asked. "It's like a banyan. Buddha sat under one all night. Wouldn't budge 'til he achieved Enlightenment. At dawn, beholding the morning star, he cried out, 'Wonderful wonderful, all beings are perfect just the way they are.'"

"I'd forgotten the story," the writer responded. "If you don't mind, I may use it."

"I thought you might."

"Thank you. But in any case, I'm no Buddha."

"*Now* you tell me."

"I mean, my trees are apt to speak for nostalgia and decay."

"Despite all that growing?"

In the ruined mill, writer looking as hard as he can, making notes, then again to the ocean to study waves. Later, he encounters an exuberantly garrulous plantation employee. Soon they're bouncing down cane roads in a company pickup, the man recounting endless tales about the plantation. Far more here than decay: another serendipity of art, and the writer feels blessed. His kind of Enlightenment.

At one site they stop, the employee teasing field-workers about waiting for a windshift before igniting the stalks. "Just burn the fucker," he yells.

"What about the E.P.A.?" a worker replies. "You know, Clean Air, that poor old lady's house over there."

The workers wait. The writer waits. "Fuck the woman and her fucking house too," his companion shouts. "And fuck the E.P.A. Tell them, 'We suck, but we do not swallow.'"

While in Hawai'i, he sends her a draft of the banyan essay, receives a letter back. "Summer is calm and dry, every sound is fragile." She encloses a Rilke poem she's translated, underlines "in the valley I am / a jubilant Jerusalem."

"I was thinking about Rilke's love life," she writes. "His resistance to involvement is the wall that protects his 'jubilant Jerusalem.'"

The last time they'd met for coffee, just before his departure, she seemed to read the writer as a kind of Rilke.

"Actually," he said, "I've lived several commitments longer than your marriage, each with many joys. Who could be comfortable with Rilke's 'What more my wife and child than visitors I could not ask to leave?'"

"You've given it some thought."

"Listen: take 'Requiem for a Friend,' Rilke's response to the death of his lover Paula. Poem notwithstanding, the ways in which he failed her were pretty ordinary. Or, his famous line, 'You must change your life.' Did he? You're writing. You'll have to think it through."

But she has. May believe that the poems redeem. Or are part of a better person than the Rilke without them. In her letter to Hawai'i, she encloses the opening of another Rilke poem: "All of you undisturbed cities, / haven't you ever yearned for the Enemy?"

Back at home, thinking about the models, the writer comes across a line from Georges Bataille suggesting that the erotic image, like eroticism itself, "exiles death." Bataille also saw eroticism as a violation, akin to death in its shock to the heart.

Later, the writer reads the observations of photographer Manuel Alvarez Bravo. "A young woman was visiting the house and we were speaking of the problems of photographing the nude. I asked her to pose for me and she accepted. When she returned, she was prepared for the sitting in a simple dress . . . at the moment she was disrobing, I asked her to pause."

Bravo also says that "Death is the ultimate nude. . . . Death removes flesh; it removes everything. All that remains are Death and the Great Nude, the bones."

# A CHAMBERED HEART

He's been to Hawai'i, returned. When they talk, she proposes taking him to a concert on his birthday. "If you don't have other obligations."

"No, no obligations."

"I can hardly believe it."

"You were surprised I wasn't seeing friends after the reading."

"Yes."

She'll be at her aunt's. The night before, however, feeling nauseous and unsettled, much as he had before leaving for Hawai'i, he calls, begs off.

"I'm disappointed," she says. He doesn't tell her how out of sorts he is, but does hear her regret. Since she'll be traveling with her husband for two weeks, then busy teaching, they schedule lunch nearly a month hence.

. . .

Little was made of birthdays when the writer was a child. He and two of his siblings had birthdays at the end of April, and his mother seemed to view three celebrations in one week as excessive. Though as an adult, the writer makes little of birthdays, this birthday and near-death-day coincide.

Frank, his doctor, asks, "You have any sense what's happening?" Such a wave of dizziness and discomfort could be cracked rib, digestive problem.

"Something's occluded."

"Why do you say that?" Frank seems unnerved.

Occlude. To close, shut, stop up. How the writer enjoys the word.

"I've never had a chance to say it before. And for sure, something weird's going on in there."

Frank nods, the writer observes, observes also that he's said something more true than he intended. Something weird *is* going on in there.

While she's gone, he nearly faints, second time in a week, leans against a building to hold on for dear life. Something deep in progress. Nausea. A throttling. Angina pectoris, a cramp in the heart.

Actually, as best as the writer can appraise what he terms his "change of heart," it's close. "Glad you're not maimed, confined to a wheelchair, or dead," a friend's physician father tells him on the phone.

Dead? Who dies at forty-nine? In good shape, surfing, lifting weights? Heavy smoker when young, but he'd quit years before, a period of bitter struggle against himself. Expensive, too: rage cost him the woman he was living with.

Then there was diet—he'd filled out, no longer thin, but fit. Or pedigree: his father's years of "heart trouble." Or the writer's nature. Restless. High-strung. Angry since birth? Expectations imposed, resisted? Choler—in ancient physiology, one of the cardinal humors, characterized by irascibility, recklessness.

So, cigarettes, diet, genetics, character—not to mention luck, cooking oil, or, the latest theory, too much testosterone. Heartquakes? Everyone has an opinion.

Now the writer learns about culverts inserted in arteries that want to collapse. About frequent failure of this procedure, Frank says, "Whether it works or not will be an act of God." A neighbor, orthopedic surgeon wired tight as a drum, argues, "Look, the heart's wrung like a sponge by stress. It takes months to unwring it, if you ever can." As for where stress comes from? "For you," the surgeon tells him triumphantly, "writing's a killer. You're writing your heart out."

Another doctor, an old friend, takes a related tack: "Writers are the canary in the mine shaft. Some don't return alive. Stress is resistance to things as they are."

"Art's not song?"

"You know what I mean."

What the writer knows. Of course, that writing is in part an argument with the world. In one aspect, a quest to change something—story; self.

The cardiologist wants to teach the writer how to live better. "Is writing hard work?" he asks, thoughtfully.

"In some regards it's straightforward labor, blue collar."

"Perhaps you should think about easing up." They study each other across the silence. "Nothing is forever."

The writer hears the cardiologist say this, records it, files it away.

Meanwhile, another question. "Do you belong to a church?"

"Is surfing a church?"

"No."

The writer recalls his parents' distaste for the professionally religious.

"Well, going to church correlates with lower incidence of coronary disease. You're a receptor. Too intense. You can be yourself and live less long. Or become someone else and live longer."

The writer grins. He's thinking, I'll be myself, only less often.

But the cardiologist's inexorable. "Also, you have to remember to ask yourself, 'Is the glass half empty or half full.'"

"Half empty or half full?" The writer says this as writer: repetition for recall.

"Half empty or half full." Doctor making it clear to patient.

As the writer departs, the cardiologist gives him a life-size model of the heart. From a pharmaceutical company. She won't believe this, he tells himself, carrying it down the corridor. When he reaches the elevator, he sees a tableau of the elderly, crippled, and maimed. Shaking his head, the writer thinks how she'll laugh when he explains, "I'm gonna be myself, but less often."

When she arrives at the cottage for lunch, she brings a videocassette she wants to give him, Saura's flamenco version of the opera *Carmen*. They're sitting on the small couch in the living room. She's been describing how Carmen refuses to give up her freedom.

"I have something to tell you," he says after a silence. "While you were away, I had a heart operation. I suppose I could have died. It was my birthday. I knew I wasn't feeling good when we spoke the night before. Anyway, this is crazy. I understand you're married, but I must tell you— I've been thinking about you all the time."

She leans toward him. Cups his face in her hands. Cups his face in her hands.

. . .

The writer's GP Frank made it sound beyond choice: "You can't be different than you are." Death knell? A friend reminds him the Fates told Achilles his life could be short and glorious or long and ordinary. Another friend dismisses the argument: life is stress, he says. And anyway there's good stress versus bad stress.

The writer weighs how much to tell her. Laughs, remembering a refrain from childhood. "That's for me to know and you to find out." Her insistent questions seem not just concern but a hunger for what she calls "back story." They feel like prying to him, but of course he recognizes the impulse, thinks again how much she's like him. Or the him he was.

One day, he reads her a newspaper article about a surfer who, struggling with cancer, surfed wave after wave one night, then tied himself to a buoy. Taking some barbiturates, the surfer planned to pass out, but not in the deep blue—afraid of sharks. In the morning, spotted by a friend teaching a surf class, he was brought in. Unconscious, but alive.

"You've never thought of doing something like that, have you?" she asks.

The writer considers telling her how depressed he's been. "You mean because I'm a surfer?"

"Please."

"I don't want to discuss it."

"Please."

"No comment."

"This isn't good. No one's ever turned me down before."

"Think of the bright side: it's a first."

"I'm going to get you for that! You imagine you have heart trouble now? I'm going to buy a dozen doughnuts. Cream-filled. Then I'm going to make you eat every last one."

The writer thinks it over. "I guess you don't like being turned down."

"You're beginning to get the picture." She pauses. Lets him beg the question.

Posthumous. Mammon at the millennium, song of stocks and bonds. Nasdaq up 80 percent in a year. One analyst opines, "This is not a mania."

Feeling pretty good, the writer asks his cardiologist for a prognosis. Too many variables for accurate predicting, he's told.

"But should I buy growth stocks or money market funds?" the writer replies.

They laugh, but that's where the conversation ends. Leaving the cardiologist's office, biking home, the writer realizes he's bearish on the future. So many drownings, drowned.

Postheart. Proust, holed up in that cork-lined room for ten years to write about the life before. Perhaps not so unusual: memory may demand an accounting. Writer selling books, putting others in the garage. A sense of what he can no longer contain in head or field of vision. A near-rage for cleaning up. Dispersing—verb his mother used when giving memorabilia to her grown children. Sifting. Spewing. Having to farewell the known to have any hope of another voyage out. This even as one reexamines, recapitulates; to move forward is a kind of vandalism.

Box of love letters—three hundred from one woman, each two or three pages single-space. You could spend weeks rereading. Reliving. Are the letters best returned? Destroyed? The writer's concerned about what he'll be leaving to be, as they say, disposed of.

Going virtual. Honolulu is full of middle-aged day traders. Heavily computerized, on-line long before dawn for the opening of the New York Exchange, these men see themselves as outlaws. Nevada postal box to avoid Hawaii taxes. Cell phones: no one knows where they are. Their phrase "exit strategy," meaning retirement planning, but the writer hears something else. Good-bye, aging alphas! Free; too free. Sadhus in India, children grown, giving up on family life, on the road begging. And, from TV, an aging water buffalo cut out from herd, hyena at hamstring.

The heart. The writer rethinks being alone. After a brutal separation, the third one of his adult life, each of which he occasioned, he has for a year now been in the cadences of his own metabolism. And, with the waning of remorse? Relief. Less scrutiny. Fewer lies, half-truths. One's own version of the story. A return to undomesticated sexual variety. Freedom to be still more possessed by his art.

And yet: according to Nancy Newhall, "When change came to Edward Weston, it nearly always took the shape of a woman." And, the writer reads in his notes, "The emissaries of necessity are all women."

# YOU UNDISTURBED CITIES

The next time they plan to see each other, she doesn't want to come to the cottage. They meet for coffee, then go down to the bay, look over to San Francisco. This is a place that for the writer bombilates with memories. The extraordinary woman he lived with in his twenties. Years spent on the derelict yacht they restored. The time they walked on the fish pier and agreed it was over. But never, never has the writer seen the shoreline so intense, shimmering: grass of the park hypergreen, sky hyperblue.

As they sit on the bench, facing the Golden Gate, he tumbles slowly to the side, head into lap, looks up into her blue eyes. She cups his cheeks in her hands, as before, and they begin to kiss. She bites his lip, hard; sucks, hard. Their mouths fit, seem made for each other.

At coffee, she'd asked whether or not he had children, or, how many. He'd teased, wouldn't answer. It seemed to mean a lot to her. But why?

Now he says, gazing up, "No children."

"I don't believe you."

He shrugs. Their eyes locked, he feels like one of Konrad Lorenz's goslings: imprinting on her. Then, utterly undoing him, she begins to unpin her long brown hair. Bathes him in a downpour. Of abundance, appetite.

Later, she opens her shoulder bag, takes out some letters. She'd spoken of an older man, an artist. It turns out they've been corresponding. His letters have been going to . . . her aunt's. That is, something she doesn't want her husband to be part of, though she's said they share everything.

The writer's heart sinks. Of course she's too seductive not to have men in the wings.

"This artist and I spoke a number of times. He's lonely in his marriage. I wanted to be true to our conversations. That's all."

"Oh."

"And that's all it will be. But I've learned something important from him. I don't want to live with regret."

"Meaning?"

"Meaning, there was a chance for love he passed by out of loyalty to his wife."

"Don't choices imply regret?"

"He feels he should have acted when love presented itself."

They sit next to each other on the bench now, quiet. The writer wonders if she imagines there won't be a price for love.

"I have something else to show you." She takes out a packet of photographs. Snapshot of her as sulky teenager. Of her and her husband rehearsing their wedding waltz. Of them at the Vermeer exhibit in Washington. The writer's dizzied; these lives pass before his eyes.

So, letters from the artist. Pictures. Writer's head in her lap, their extraordinary kissing. Something guileless about all this. Trusting. As if she's counting on him to do the right thing. To care for her as a parent would. As if she'll be another of his many children.

She calls. "I need to hear your voice." She pauses. "I don't want to do damage to my husband. If we go further, I won't be able to see you again."

"I understand. But we're very drawn to each other. You know that."

"Yes."

Sound of their breathing.

"Want to hear a story?" he asks.

"Please."

"Once upon a time . . ."

She laughs.

"Once upon a time . . . there was a writer, and he was smitten by desire for an amazing young woman. He was old enough to be her father."

"Yes."

"And she was attracted to him."

"Yes."

"And he said to her, 'We'll work it out together, I know we can.'"

"Yes."

"And she said yes to him, though she thought it was wrong, and foolish, too."

"Yes," she replies. "I like that story."


She calls again. "I want to take care of you."

"Please do."

"I'm just calling so you know where I am."

"I'm glad you did."

"I'm very confused."

"Let me help."

"I don't know if I can do this."

"Dear one, I can help."

"Yes. You'll have to help me."

. . .

All I have is my sensibility," she tells him.

He thinks of her love of lieder's sumptuous melancholy. *Sehnsucht*, pining for the unattainable.

"You and I will not spend our lives together." She says this as if, as if it were written. "We don't share the same fate."

He notes the word, though she later says it's only that one time she's used it, just with him. He's thinking the word too big for lives like theirs. Self-aggrandizing. Over-determined. Florid. This despite sex/love/lust, among other monosyllables he's had to acknowledge to be true.

"Et cetera," he adds, stopping himself from continuing the list.

She comes in the front door, pulls him to the bedroom, tears at his clothes. So rabid, her hunger almost seems to have nothing to do with him, is true to itself, period. To what she's talked herself into.

She's moaning, drawing him up on her, clawing at him. She's going to Give Herself To Him.

"Take me," she says.

How anachronistic, he thinks. Nor has he ever liked the imperative. He feels she's absorbed in her own drama, and why not, but for a moment sees the two of them from a great distance. Then, letting his body decide, he does what she wants. What they both want.

# AS IF POSSESSED

She's moving at what seems to him double or triple time, writhing, bucking. Under, on, around him. He almost laughs—she may make him seasick.

He holds her face in his hands. "Stop, stop. We're in it together."

"We are?"

"Let me help. Please."

"All right."

"There you go. Poor thing."

"Why poor thing?"

"I've taken advantage of you. I'm older."

"Yes. Wicked man."

Later, she asks, "Am I repressed?" Her experience is

limited, he's to play the Casanova, but is sure she knows the answer.

"Well, am I?"

"I think not."

"What else do you think?"

"Well, we're quite something together."

"Quite something? Faint praise. Anyway, you tell that to everyone."

"No. I don't."

And doesn't. Hasn't. But how explain, for example, the rue he felt when she leaned over to take him in her mouth. Of course she'd done it before. Call me old-fashioned, he thinks. And then, Oh come on, you're a bit old for rue.

Giving in to the giving. The taking.

Lying next to her, he marvels. Still alive. A thought that evokes, from twenty years before, the day his father died. No surprise: it periodically returns to him, not, he feels, as memory, but as problem to be solved. Perhaps if he can only narrate it correctly?

There was a woman—an acquaintance—he'd bumped into that morning two decades ago, a nurse, who seemed to care, to be able to care, only for those in jeopardy. Since he was in good health, and fairly happy—wanting only more love, like just about everybody—they were unlikely to know each other better. But that evening, learning his father had died, waiting for the plane in the morning, not knowing what else to do, he called her.

This almost-stranger gave him wine, glass after glass, then guided him to bed, helped him undress. Joined him under the covers. For a moment he was back to childhood: mulberry tree in front yard; blind friend at summer camp; Houdini-the-cat stuck up on the roof; siblings loving, bickering. Chorus in grammar school singing, "I lift my lamp . . ." And then, restored somehow across distance and time, he was in her as she looked up at him, quite calm, as if what they were doing was exempt from argument.

I'm astonished," she says.

"Why?"

"Not telling." Mock-childish. Saucy, impudent.

Can he guess? He thinks he's at times known one person well, then, over the years with different lovers, glimpsed the universal—women—before working back to some understanding of this one human being, that. Nonetheless, there's a great distance in age between them. And, these days, he's keenly aware of what he didn't know when he thought he did.

Still, he'd guess she's looking at her own body as if it's a stranger's. Doing things as if it has a mind of its own. As if it, and at least part of her will, could take her where she's hardly sure the woman she's been wants to go.

As for himself, he's determined to try to convey to her what he feels. Certain she thinks he's gone through it all before; afraid he'll never see her again as soon as she decides the threat to her marriage is too great.

Where to begin? He tries to tell her he's been transformed by his heart episode, as he was, years before, by his mother's death. That their pleasure and passion amaze him. Their delirium.

What to do? When they're together, say, after they make love and more love, he asks, "Have I told you today how much I desire you?"

"No. You haven't. Terrible man."

When his mother died, ten years after his father, the writer was again single. The preceding several years, he'd spent time with various women. More than once, almost by accident, becoming the lover of an old friend or acquaintance. Interested, informed, as ties sexualized in contexts he'd not expected.

Separated from the woman he'd loved, in any case, still he spoke with her often. They were family. Not surprisingly, after his mother's death she came to see him. And, as whenever they met, it was in the air that they might make love.

So there they were, at his parents' apartment, and to him she was still beautiful. Though much mayhem—and regret—had passed between them, there was loyalty, and rich memory of what they'd shared in their pursuit of life on water when they'd been a tribe of two.

Time for bed. Orphaned: parents gone. They lay next to each other, embraced. She felt him become aroused, looked down.

"Like alabaster," she said, pulling him closer.

I want to die in your arms," she tells him. No fear of extravagance.

"You want to die?"

"No. I mean, I'm so happy I could die now."

"I prefer life," he replies.

Ecstasy. The real. There can be fidelity, the richly shared ordinary, honored obligation. These, she feels, can receive the highest attention, evolving into the treasured. But sustained passion of this kind?

Ecstasy. Together, they lose track of time, each memory-obliterating renewal of desire, a shadow story refusing to end. They remember, sometimes only days later, specifics of what passed between them. But in the moment or hours themselves, they are a continuum, undifferentiated. "You're more than the sum of your parts," he says. She isn't sure how much of a compliment he's offered. And he's amused by the backhandedness; the tease. But it is a fact that she's more than the sum of any one feature or quality: the whole is shape-changing, changes him. She loves to put her hand on him after he comes. "Take your hand off my vulva," he tells her, and they both laugh. Sometimes it is hard to figure out who's who, where one ends, the other begins.

How she talks, feels. "You made me weep," she says, torn. Or, "I almost fainted." ("Almosts don't count," he responds.) And then, of course, there are souls. Souls? Souls. Not to mention the divine.

"I thought you were a god," she tells him. On their knees, he's behind, using strength and weight to push her down on forearms, pinning wrists with hands. She's shifting, pitching, pulling, trying to rise.

"Ouch," he says. Something pinched.

A dancer, so flexible; infant who can suck her toes. She rotates to stare at him. Baby owl. There's a painting by Ingres, *The Grand Odalisque.* Oh, the brouhaha this painting caused. Critics arguing the unclothed female figure has too many vertebrae. Elongated back, haunch, *enhaunchement:* distortion of female anatomy. But Ingres knew what he wanted. Needs are complex, they say. Whichever—at that moment she turns round toward him.

"I thought you were a god," she says. "Now I realize you're just a man wearing the mask of a god."

. . .

Y ou're too Greek for me," she tells him. As if the writer's a living argument about seizing the moment. For the ancients, no salvation, no repetition, just the precarious beauty of the here and now.

Too Greek. At twenty-one, the writer went to law school for ten days, then quit. Imagined there was only one right choice for the rest of his life, that he had to make it then. Believed—and in this she sounds like him—his soul was in danger. Back in Cambridge, he met a grad student looking to share an apartment. This fellow had just directed a college production of Euripides' *Bacchae*. Taught the cast ancient Greek, played the part of the king, did the choreography. Beyond *The Bacchae*, his priorities were François Villon, Fats Waller, Bach. Lay on the floor, weeping, when the writer got him high on marijuana as they listened to the *Magnificat*.

Having dropped out of law school to save his soul, the writer read *The Bacchae*. You know how the story goes: Dionysius and his rowdy followers come to town; the king, Pentheus, all law and order, disrespects the god, who has perhaps taken the form of one of his sexually ambiguous followers; the local women go mad. The king's mother, inspired (and so blinded), tears her son limb from limb. Sex, murder. One frenzy, another. The writer has a picture of his friend, twenty, playing Pentheus. As Pentheus, face contorted. The writer looks at the photograph: agony, and, now, nearly thirty years later, all that will not recur.

Gifts of the gods. Dionysius, who seduces, makes moist. Does not coerce; induces hallucinations. For the ancient Greeks, the bumper sticker might have read, TRANSFORMA-TION HAPPENS. Madness, but also an end of the ordinary.

"I'm in danger," she says. Impelled to flight; transfixed. Fearful of prices to be paid, wounds inflicted, she seems to feel she's living up to her true self, has located her own story. Enchanted by it as much as by what they are together.

The end of the ordinary. Speaking of his parents' deaths, the writer tells her they have no graves. Wanted no graves. Ashes strewn. A very ethical agnostic, and lover of language, his physician father was once asked by a priest if he considered the remission of a cancer a miracle. Having seen many inconsolable deaths, the writer's father was deeply sympathetic to the hunger for explanation. But, true to his beliefs, could respond only that any such remission was of course "miraculous."

In matters of faith, the writer's his parents' child. No religious observance, though he did once hear himself thanking Something or Someone for the beauty of another day out on the (warm) ocean. He's also experienced frequent joy in the physical self-in-the-world. And often been intense, exhilarated, striving. If then confused, depressed. But in a state of wonder? As he is now?

. . .

How things get complex. To herself, she says, "No," which means not possible; never. To herself, she argues, "Perhaps," or "Just once," because . . . it seems more wrong to deny this truth. Or: she's suddenly, ravenously curious. Knows she can carry it off. Is certain nothing can threaten her marriage. Or, spoiled by her spouse, his trust/dependence/indulgence, feels it can be done. Shouldn't be done. Must be done.

To the writer she says, finally, "Yes," though it's just this one time, then "Yes," then "Yes" again, because after a while, when this is a first or that is a first—the time the melting takes place, or when they both achieve the surface, gasping, or when her hand comes up from under, or something as simple as her lips waiting, again so close he's out of focus, his hands lifting, holding her there . . . or when she explains what was vital to make clear: that's who she is, yes, but only with him . . . because then, though she doesn't intend it/doesn't want it/doesn't really ask for it (even as she demands nothing less, knows no other way to be), because then, when they're "in it together," he's "the most beautiful thing" that's ever happened to her.

"You're my cosmos," she tells him, so pleased with herself. His "vain woman," his "beautiful baby."

# DEEPER

Her sensibility, journey to their first meeting. Pain, sorrow. Self-invention. Story she tells herself; story the writer hears. He pictures, is intended to picture, an almost princess, a faraway land. Precocious child, enamored reader. The man known as Father is good to her, teaches her to read and write, early, but dies when she's five. Later, the mother's captured by evil forces. Daughter alone in the castle, except for an aged servant. But she does have art, books in particular, many in translation. Andersen's *The Little Mermaid. Dr. Zhivago.* Matthew Arnold's "Dover Beach": "Ah, love, let us be true / To one another! . . . And we are here as on a darkling plain."

So there the girl is, fifteen, sixteen, alone in the castle in that faraway land. "Small and run-down," she explains.

"Grotty, to use the English-English word." Empty rooms, paintings and jewelry long since sold off. Heirloom harp, billiard table: gone. Her dark brown hair long, longer, heart full of stories of yearning, separation. Even more alone because she's young for her grade in school(!). Doesn't get along with her classmates. Can't talk about her mother's captivity.

Finally, her mother's released, but fails to return. Has disappeared, been disappeared. Soon she joins her aunt in a new land. Secretly marries, not telling her aunt, who knows her ward deserves better—they're nobility. But she does marry, this devoted spouse to whom she is devoted. Makes a religion of her marriage, she says. "An absolute commitment." When she and the writer first meet, he feels he's never encountered anyone more married. Save, perhaps, his mother.

It could be the writer's sense of his mother and this young woman as kin—beyond lieder, beyond the late adolescent battle for the Beloved, beyond the wit—is confirmed here. Or in the search for a nomenclature of their relationship.

"I can only love someone," she says, "not be their lover."

Not a lover. Weighing alternatives. She's his mother? Well, no, though she wants to care for him.

What then? Might he adopt her? This makes them laugh: he can introduce her as his daughter. What could be more legitimate? Allow, demand, ongoing connection.

The pillow talk of others: you had to be there. Nonetheless . . . "Indulge me," as she says. And of course the writer must, will. He's her father, is he not? "Please indulge me." It's the "please" he finds irresistible. Another time, it's, "May I not be allowed to dream?"

Once, as they finish making love, she's beaming, looking down.

"I almost proposed," she says, glowing with happiness.

"What were the words?"

"You will love me forever."

"That's almost proposing?"

"I'm your daughter. It's not my fault."

Nomenclature. Genealogy. If he's her father, who's her mother? Perhaps she was discovered in a basket on her (seeming) parents' doorstep, a foundling. But baby's jealous. Who did he sleep with? Something they'll have to work out, with counseling, perhaps.

Meanwhile, her over-the-top hyperbole. Might be contagious, the writer tells himself.

My dearest, my love. My man. My heart. And—think about someone saying it to you, apparently meaning it— my king. My lord and master. As in, "My lord and master, I have to go home now."

.   .   .

Forty-nine. The writer laughs at the thought: what they call comparables in real estate. An aspect of his own aging—all women now have a penumbra, evoke someone once known. Glint of eye, story told, lilt of voice, Grand Plan for the future, curve of breast. He feels this most with the models, perhaps because it's a way of beginning to organize the data each so intensely presents as she sits in his study.

As for precursors of his daughter? Perhaps one. Intelligent, verbal, well read. Seductive, coy, breathless, highstrung, never less than deeply moved. Lived at a distance. Sent postcards: Weston shell; Botticelli's *Birth of Venus*; Cranach's *Eve.* Would drop to her knees when they were reunited, hands on his Levi's. How they both loved such flair!

Married, she'd also loved—and made love to—a woman, dreamed of those breasts "deeper" than her own. Wanted the writer, to tell him these stories, wanted his child. To get spanked, have her face slapped: eros of being contrary, disciplined. The writer, thirty, newly single, was shocked, even as she taught him what he needed to know. Compelled by her, still he found her too difficult, never felt the sympathy or impulse to protect his daughter now elicits. Said, finally, relentlessly, "No, I'm sorry, but I can't."

．　．　．

$M$aster." Provenance? The elusive female object of desire in a novel she's reading uses the word. This is very much his long-lost and newfound daughter. Why be chary? "Poeticize" as pejorative? She's unfazed.

"People talk about dangers of reading," she tells the writer. "They say we'll want a given story, or one like it, to happen to us. Francesca and Paolo in *The Inferno*, the doomed lovers, are seduced by reading a medieval romance. The folly of believing too much in art." She laughs. "But what about not believing enough in art? The too-prudent. The careerist. Who will claim that story as his own?"

"Her own," the writer says. "Equal pronouns, please."

The writer's disputatious daughter. The writer listens. Understands she really does believe we're no less than the song we (dare to) sing. As he did at her age.

$H$ow does it all begin? One morning, having spent the night—allegedly at her aunt's—she stays in bed when he goes out for coffee. He returns with a mocha topped with whipped cream.

"Wake up, baby." Leans over, nuzzles her cheek. "Here's

mocha for the tired baby. For the baby-who-doesn't-get-up baby. For the beautiful baby."

She turns, yawns, stretches. "For the most beautiful baby?"

"For the spoiled baby. For the brash and flamboyant baby. For the baby-baby."

"Mmm," she says, turning, rising to take the cup. "I am the baby-baby."

The baby-baby. Holding and withholding. Leading and misleading. Leaving and relieved.

In loco parentis. Loco, not for the first time, the writer asks himself what kind of father he'll be. Indulgent? Absent? Domineering? Codependent? Sugar-daddied?

To baby and be babied. Paternal rescue—the man she calls Father is gone from the castle when she's five. And for the writer as newborn father, to almost die—and what's come to seem a lifetime's withholdings—leaves him willing, able, to lose himself in her.

"Dear one," he tells her, "at this rate I could end up changing your diapers." She nods. Smiles.

The baby's job, evolutionists argue, is to get the protection it needs. Anything making it more adorable has been selected for over thousands of years. Children thus seducing the parent into being willingly consumed, parents subordinating their own hungers to the baby's drive never to be abandoned.

Care. Psychologists say the daughter expects the father to save her, most of all from the consequences of her desire to seduce and be seduced by him, to have him seduce and be seduced by her.

The baby, the baby-baby. How clever of her, to be his daughter. His only child, to answer her early question. How could she have known he'd be so powerfully moved?

The writer also has this sense: if they separate, she'll never have a father again.

My Zeus." She's reading Graves on Greek myths, Fagels's translation of *The Odyssey.* The writer bellowed as they came: Zeus. Baby litmus, immersed in what she reads, moved (at least briefly), transformed. Also, Zeus gives birth to his own children—Athena from his head, Dionysius from his thigh, and so on. "That's why I'm part of you," she says triumphantly. "I'm not even the daughter of my mother."

Of course the writer's pleased she's happy with this, though it does give him pause: too close to a god, mortals get not just transfigured but burned. Still, Athena's not at risk, he supposes. This possibility comes up once she begins to see him as Odysseus, the man whose name is trouble. Perhaps Athena, protector of Odysseus, is something more than just a goddess to that wily man.

"Or," he says, "maybe you're Odysseus. The baby Odysseus."

She laughs. "I know what you mean. I'm the trickster

telling stories. And, despite the enchantments of this cottage, the one always heading home."

The writer shakes his head. Again amazed that she can experience such passion, then depart. Not that he hasn't done something similar more than once.

"Nothing you haven't done," she tells him, as if reading his mind.

If you're the baby," he says, "what's that in your hands? A bottle?"

"Not bad."

"Then what?"

"Baby's rattle."

"Very good."

"I love you," she says.

"That's a first."

"Yes."

"Took quite a while."

"Now it's untrue not to say it."

"Come here and kiss your father."

"Can't you see I'm busy?"

Later, they watch a video. The writer remembers the film from three decades before, saw it several times, read the screenplay. *Les Enfants du paradis*. Four men in love with one woman, aloof and elusive Garance. The mime Baptiste is the man she loves, will be with only one night.

Upstairs, they arrange the pillows, unfold some blankets, tuck themselves in, watch for about twenty minutes. She's spellbound. Then, abruptly, the writer picks up the remote, presses the OFF button.

"Sorry, I can't take it."

"What?"

"The inevitable loss."

More true, her joy in watching it reminds him how much—how many things not him—make her happy. As they go down to bed, she seems unperturbed.

"I'll rent it again soon," he says. "I apologize."

Several weeks later, he gets the film when she's away, once more captivated at the finale, Baptiste calling after Garance as she vanishes in the carnival crowd. None of the four men who love her will ever possess her.

Soon after, she tells him she saw the video the previous night. Doesn't have to add that she watched it with her husband.

In the cardiac emergency unit, the word *catheter*. One of those words that, over the years, the writer hadn't liked the sound of, knocked on wood about. When, say, a friend had kidney stones, recounted his morphine misery. Urethra; pipe; bladder. And the writer's memory, incompletely blocked, of his mother, dying, catheterized.

Words. This catheter turns out to be no more than a condom attached to a hose and bottle. Good news. But . . . should the writer have trouble urinating, they'll invoke the other kind. Which is the reason, in the dead of night, wired to monitors, hospital gown pulling apart, the writer struggles to sit up.

Bells, whistles, alarms, nurse running in.

"What are you doing?"

"I'm trying to overcome an inability to urinate uphill."

The nurse laughs, steadies him. Stands waiting. Both of them waiting. He thinks of his mother, propped up in a wheelchair, head sagging.

"Hold on," the nurse finally says. Going over to the sink, she spins both handles, water gushing. *Woosh:* sympathetic response.

"Thank you," the writer says. "I should have thought of that, I'm a waterman." A shiver as he finishes, the familiar reflex.

Water. Years earlier, he returns to warm ocean to heal his spirit, to be overwhelmed by something larger than the human. For the last decade and more now, the writer's made warm ocean part of his annual cycle. Water, great truth-teller. Austere, opulent. Soothing, dangerous. Also, in it, the eros of solitude. Sex and ocean. Ocean as unconscious, maternal, mistress. As regression.

"My baby ocean," he calls her, all ebb and flow, though she can't swim, is afraid of drowning in him. Still keeps being drawn to them together, into the deep. Sometimes, lying on his back when he's prone, she surfs him, pubic mound pushing, pushing. As the poet Rumi argues, if the ocean were not in love, it would come to rest.

The ocean of love. Analyst Sandor Ferenczi, a contemporary of Freud's, believed we once lived in the sea, the great catastrophe being not flood but desiccation. Thus, the species developed the phallus as an effort "to restore the lost mode of life in a moist milieu."

Her moist milieu. Like all bodies of water, she requires not only mastery but surrender.

Young Hal. Twenty-two, son of old friends. The writer first met him several . . . lifetimes ago, Hal no more than a twinkle in his parents' eyes. Their next encounter was a few months later. Hal's mother was, it seemed to the writer, putting on weight. They were at the hot springs in a ranching community in the Sierra, out in the middle of nowhere. Summer nights cold, morning ground fog swaddling the peaks of barn roofs. The extraordinary woman the writer then lived with: a summer of lightning storms, of cumulus clouds paralleling the valley floor.

So, the writer thought Hal's mother was putting on weight when he saw her naked in the hot springs. Told her. She said nothing; smiled—Mona Lisa, Mona Lisa. Young Hal en route.

Twenty-two years later, after the writer's heart episode, Hal stops by the cottage. Home from college on vacation. Majoring, the writer's teased, in rap, tai chi, and kung fu. On the phone with his daughter, the writer tells Hal to sit in a lotus position in the living room. When the writer emerges from his study, there Hal is: lotus position. Hal, he realizes, can help. And so they get into meditating together. What's best is that Hal's no proselytizer. True, he tries to do things mindfully, care with what he eats, for example, but seems also to grasp he's got it made. Parents not demanding he take a job during college. Their gift of a used pickup, with insurance. Still, Hal's more than lucky: he's responded by being happy. Is willing to help the writer learn something of what he's learned.

When they meditate, the writer, breathing, breathing, still is lost in the world of maya, illusion. Often has trouble getting deeper, as it were, than his daughter. Once, when he and his young guru are doing a walking meditation—in Hal's system, meaning no task except not to hurry—they pass a teeming garden. Stop. Hummingbird's darting iridescence. Spider's homemade chandelier. Taking in the profusion of flowers, the writer cups one, stem between fingers. Inhales.

"Hal," the writer says, "this is like the sweetness of a young woman I know."

Several feet away, Hal bends over a flower, cups it, stem between fingers. Inhales.

"No, Hal," the writer tells him, suffused with happiness, "not that flower, this one."

They talk about his daughter somehow stealing away to Honolulu, but she can't. He goes alone.

Days shortening. Trade winds blowing. Cold, too: must have been 65 last night. The writer could see the narrow lower lip of light of the new moon falling toward the horizon, suggestion of disc barely visible above. New moon. A true thing. Lucky to witness it. Or the Pleiades, that celestial bouquet.

Now, first light, time to paddle out. Wet-suit vest, wet-suit jacket for a second layer against sitting and, no doubt, waiting, baseball cap against thermal loss. At forty-nine, postheart, forget vanity: stay warm.

Dawn, high tide, not a soul at these breaks just offshore a city of almost a million. Heading out the channel, no turtles, frigate birds not yet soaring—sleeping in, or waiting for thermals. Whales due in their annual commute. Writer stopping to sit up, look around. Humans. Question: what did the ocean come before? Thinking also of the wings of white hair on his chest, as if airbrushed in. (How she loves them.) A keen sense, yesterday, watching teenagers at sunset riding the trade-wind swell, that after the self is gone there will still be waves, surfers taking those waves. But of course.

This reef break—Suicides. Near several other breaks—Old Man's, Rice Bowl. Naming: Suicides—don't forget to kick out before the inside reef. As for this morning, it's not just small but blown down. So why be there? Oh, well, for the exercise. Or, to get that far from the madness on shore. To be in the born-again morning light, darkness only a memory.

And: suddenly, outside a set seems to be forming. A set? The writer gets paddling. Up and over the first wave, scanning the second as it begins to rise. Pivots, pulls with both arms, then on his feet as he and the board move forward and down, and, what do you know, once again the . . . miraculous.

Long ride. Losing the force, finally, close to shore. The writer turns, not eager to make the effort to go back out. Sits, looks around. Diamond Head: flanks and crevices still in shadow.

Breathing deep, letting out a long exhale, the writer rises and falls on the swell. Thinks of his baby ocean.

# WORK OF ART

Ovid's Pygmalion, "shocked at the vices of women . . . chose to live alone / To have no woman in his bed." Pygmalion then carves a statue of a woman. Falls in love with it. Responding to his prayers, Venus intervenes; the statue comes alive. Some say the impulse to create such images derives from unsatisfiable longing. Or, perhaps, from grieving.

The writer's daughter eagerly takes pictures, thinks she's good at it, is good at it. Also likes pictures taken of her, beguiled by the multiplicity of selves. All this resonates with one of the writer's early emotions after they meet—he's afraid of losing her before he can articulate to himself her most frequent aspects. Some weeks after they begin making love, after she's held the camera at arm's length to take pictures of them together, after she's asked someone in a café to take a picture of them with her camera, he tells her he's going to buy a Polaroid. Says he's never used one.

"Same here," she replies. Nor has she modeled, though she does give him a picture of herself, in lingerie top, staring sultrily at the lens. At her husband.

A few days later he shows her the new camera. She laughs—he's relentless! Then shrugs. Not something she'd have initiated? Perhaps she feels no more than a willingness to see the photos if he insists. But also seems to read the camera as a dare: he wouldn't be thinking she's afraid, would he?

"Do whatever you want."

As if to prove she trusts him to have the photos in his possession. How else justify their lovemaking, what she's betraying? As she herself cannot be trusted. Or perhaps it all turns on giving him something in return for all she intends to withhold.

At the start, the picture taking is almost prim. Perhaps because he doesn't want her to say no. Thinks she has reason to. That he'd decline were he her. Or because he has little idea what he's doing, despite the models—where he wants to go, how to go there. Or perhaps she conveys her own inexperience, reservations, sense of propriety.

The kitchen table. They've just taken yet another bath after making love. Click, flash, a whirring as print ejects.

Slowly, the first image clarifies. Her chest, gold chain, his left hand on her left breast, nipple above his index finger, his thumb along the upcurve, his left forearm running back toward the camera. Her right arm resting on the kitchen table. Slice of salami between her thumb and forefinger.

Similarly, the second photo at the table is between neck and waist. Torso, breasts, now also belly button and waist, edge of black towel. His left forearm extends toward her left breast. Her right hand is more clear—the salami, too! Manuscript pages on table, cup of orange juice; wicker chair.

Having thus begun, the photographer leans back. Two shots take in her face, gold chain, gold cross now very visible, mane of brown hair falling onto the right breast, down behind her neck and left shoulder. She holds one arm up, hand on her head, perhaps because he asked her to? She's calm, smiling, stares right at him-the-camera. There is also her throat, neck, hollows of her collarbones.

They sit at the kitchen table, side by side. Eating. Four photos.

The next Polaroids. In the tub, yet another bath, still chaste, perhaps because the great leap has been in the yes the photos require, or perhaps because for all the lovemaking that precedes them she's unattached to him, seeing their time together as crazy or amazing but, still and all, an interlude. Something she's having, needs. (How aware she seems of the process of becoming herself.) But nothing to derail her, particularly given her marriage. Two separate domains: different order, rank, importance. She's had to talk herself into coming here, this experience is absolutely true, has required passionate response. But no more than that.

So, the tub. He's at eye level; she faces the camera, one breast showing, the other obscured by the dictionary, which rests on the rim of the tub. Tile behind. In another photo, he's closer; she's smiling at his approach. Below, pubic hair under the surface. Then two more shots, from a greater distance. She's looking down, reading. Tap running. In all these pictures, her long hair's up, chopstick holding it in place.

Dictionary. She reads aloud: " 'Clavicle: either of two slender bones each articulating with the sternum and a scapula and forming the anterior part of a shoulder.' " She laughs. "Listen. The clavicle's connected to the acromion, humeras, radius, ulna, carpus, metacarpal, and phalanx. Such beautiful words."

In several other tub photos, she's either inspecting a shot just taken or brandishing it for his inspection. In another, a hand—hers—fingers spread, rests on her belly, a second hand, also hers, on her chest as she reclines. He can just make out the wedding ring. And, finally, standing up now, she's drying her face, blue eyes peering over the towel's vertical black and white stripes.

Prisoner of love? Oh, no: she's simply had enough of the camera for one day.

Semi-Olympia, the writer's daughter calls it. A photo he looks at many times. This is some weeks after the table and tub Polaroids. They've been making love for hours, on the bed, on the floor. Exhausted, having "fallen off the horse," as she puts it, she lies on her back on the blue cotton quilt. Pillow, box of film, Navajo rug. Rug and pillow doubled in the wall mirror beside her. She and the writer in the mirror, using the mirror. She watches him enter her from behind, accelerates madly with him as they watch. They're of the same mind and body in this, driven by what they see. "Oh, look at us," she shouts.

She shouts, but also possesses a reserve his mother would have applauded. One night, the moon full, he brings her out to the front yard. When he starts to undress, she is, if not shocked, unsettled. "Someone will see me," she says. He knows better, knows the fences, sight lines, but she's unconvinced.

Someone will see. This photo on the blue quilt: she's supine, looking at him. A languid "do what you will" expression. Thighs in foreground, legs slightly apart. Pubic hair, passion-rouged labia. Hips, torso, breasts, armpits are beyond, arms up and back behind her head. Marks on her arms. Bite marks. Her expression is to and for him, as if the camera doesn't intervene. She's there, he's there, they're there, postcoital, sated, dazed. But both of them want this picture, want the anticipated moment of shared viewing. Have the technology and will to take it.

His daughter admires Duras's *The Lover*, gives him a copy. Adolescent French girl, older Chinese lover. Looking back, the (adult woman) narrator describes a classmate's breasts: "She bears them unknowingly, and offers them for hands to knead, for lips to eat . . . I'd like to eat Hélène Lagonelle's breasts as he eats mine."

Gifts. The video she gave the writer, Saura's flamenco *Carmen*. In one scene there's a dance class, all women. They sweep back and forth in unison, a flock, a school. "Your breasts are like the horns of the bull," the woman teacher tells the students.

"These are my jewels, you can't." She says this the first time he reaches for her breasts. Down at the bay. Married. Some months later, looking into the mirror, she says, "Oh, see my nipples!" They watch her breasts as he enters her. She's leaning forward, his hands cupping from behind. Or, with her astride, her hands placing his on her breasts. He pulls her nipples, hard. Harder.

"I love your breasts," he says. "They're very hopeful."

He begins to suck a nipple, then tries to take in the entire breast. It becomes clear she's awakened something long unrequited. Larkin's "deep loss restored."

"Careful," the writer tells her later, head cradled on her chest. "Only a sick puppy would do that."

"Do what?"

"Be so voracious." He pauses. "Ingest. Verb."

They look it up. To take or put food, etc., into the body. "Oh well," he says; it misses the desperation. Then, remembering a college psychology course's neo-Freudian rhetoric, adds, "Breast withheld, breast proffered."

"Here," she says, giving him a nipple.

Later, she suggests they look up *catenary,* a noun. She leafs through the dictionary, then reads aloud: "'curve assumed by a cord or chain freely hanging from two points not in the same vertical line.'" She grins. "Can you see it?"

The writer thinks again about Rodin, thousands of sketches of nudes: female body as flower, torso as stem. "The smiling of the breasts," Rodin said. And, yes, how her breasts make the writer smile. In one picture they take with her camera—shot acceptable to a photo lab—they see what the lens perceived, what the eye did not. Nipples, hard, pushing at fabric. Her breasts. Sun, sphere. Enticing in themselves; and beautiful in a camisole bought on sale: his come-hither baby is frugal, too.

Sometimes, with her in his mouth, he looks up, sees hand massaging breast. Nipple between thumb and forefinger, or fingers kneading.

"That's what I'd do if I were you," he tells her. And, as if it followed, "You're the woman I'd be if I were a woman." And, more of the obvious, "You're more me than I would be, if I were you."

"Why so surprised?" She laughs. "Everyone yearns for the lost unity with another being that preceded birth. Thus incessant, unappeasable desire to find one's other part. But you, my father, you've heard this before."

The writer lifts his head. "I have?"

"My Zeus. It was your idea. Bisecting those insolent, four-legged, two-faced original human creatures. Leaving each half yearning, embracing in never-ending hunger."

The drive north: overnight trip to a cabin by the ocean, perhaps the only one they'll ever make. She brings her camera. The next morning, the writer's lying on the bed before they depart, wearing his black watch cap, black T-shirt, jeans, vest. Mustache layered with white, wrinkles at the corners of his eyes, wicker headboard behind, head on pillow. Hands folded, fingers interlaced, yielding as he looks at the photographer. Exhausted, but happy.

Back home at the cottage, he's on the stairs by those sex and death books, torso bare, wearing jeans. "Wait," she says, and gets her camera. Again, he's staring at her, open to whatever the photographer desires.

When they get the prints, he's startled. As if at the moment of the picture he's looking out at someone who understands him and (nonetheless?) values him, someone on the verge of making him smile once again. Who sees him as he wants to be. He also thinks, studying the prints, that three months earlier they hadn't slept together. Remembers the hospital.

The day she took these pictures, after using her camera she picked up the Polaroid, studied the page of operating instructions. "My father, do you mind taking off those jeans?"

"Done. Okay?"

"Not quite. It's about the underpants. And socks? I have a picture in mind."

Writer, irritated, emptying his desk drawer. Going through Xeroxes of academic papers she's written, letters, cards. Envelopes of photographs of them. Articles she's given him. He's remembered a photograph of his daughter in wedding dress, that secret ceremony. Wants to see it.

Searches and searches, but just cannot find it. Finally, always meticulous, is no longer sure whether he ever had it. Much less why it suddenly means so much to him.

As for the pictures before him: from that trip to the ocean, several wonderful images of her. Though no photographer, he simply held the camera after she set it, let her arrange herself, pressed a button. In one, she's on the deck of the cabin, wearing a low-cut black dress, with hand on hip, hair slicked down. Feline. "Very edible," he says to her, when they see the photos, and she seems to agree.

From that same weekend, a sequence of Polaroids she hates. Back at the cottage at trip's end, both of them worn out, she's wearing one of his cotton bathrobes. Lying on the bed, eyes shut, breast exposed. She sees him with the camera, pulls the robe closed. Protests as he continues. Says, finally, "You monster. Do whatever you like."

Again the dictionary.

"What are you looking up?" he asks.

"*Scrutiny.*"

"Intense examination, gaze. What about it?"

"It says 'cf scrotum.'"

"Scrotum?" The writer shakes his head. "Who knows? Maybe the impulse to gaze began with inspection of essential differences."

Words, images. She picks up the camera. He's on his back, looking at the lens; in the mirror by the bed, his double stares at her, black bra with gold trim beside him on white pillow. Black sleep mask pushed up on his forehead like Snoopy's goggles. Zeus? Again the quite mortal model.

Later, sifting through the Polaroids they've just taken, he laughs.

"What is it?" She comes in with a tray of scotch, salami, bagels, chocolate chip cookies. All of which she'll consume.

"When culture critics interrogate this photo years from now, one question will be, 'Was he naked or nude?' You're the art historian. Well?"

"An oral exam?"

"Shame on you."

"All right. For Kenneth Clark, naked is without clothes; nude is art. Body regulated, idealized. Matter into form. John Berger counters that to be naked is to be oneself; nude is to be seen by others, hence used. I myself like Anne Hollander's repudiation of any 'natural' state of unadorned humans: we always see counterimages, 'ghosts of absent clothes.' And for T. J. Clark, a nude is a 'dreamy offering of self.' He was talking of paintings of women viewed by men. And Edward Snow—patience, please—Snow said Degas's bathers articulated his need to, and I quote, 'redeem sexual desire by transforming it, through art, into a reparative impulse.' End quote."

"You memorized these phrases?"

"Grad school, my father. But listen, one more point.

About Laura Kipnis, whose *Bound and Gagged* I pulled down from your shelf that first visit to the cottage. Kipnis has fun arguing that fantasies are not necessarily desires."

"Meaning?"

"Meaning we want to ask, for instance, who's identifying with whom in any kind of looking."

"So what about this photo of me?"

"Well, take the power issues. Note the black mask. You're the object."

"Young woman exploiting helpless older man?" The writer rolls over, facedown. Several moments pass. He turns his head. "I await your efforts to console."

"Yes, my father. Coming. I'm just deciding whether you're a fantasy or a desire."

Her hair is up and back in a bun. Eyeliner, eye shadow, lipstick. Black underpants, heels. That's it. Elegant, he thinks, and sleek. Baby otter.

They face the wall mirror. He's in his Levi's, black T-shirt, Nikes. He kneels, she stands behind, holding the Polaroid under his chin, wrists on his shoulders, left breast obscured by his head, right breast just beyond his right ear.

In another exposure she leans forward, most of her torso behind his head and back, flash again going off in front of his chest. Her slight smile: affection, yes, but she set up the shot. Knows it's going to be good.

# IN IT TOGETHER

Y̶ou're so young," he says one night. "Where's the rest of you?"

They're drinking single malt. Writer sobered by her capacity to down it, though she professes never to have had anything stronger than wine.

"*Fyxen*," he explains, "Anglo-Saxon, becomes *fixen* in Middle English. Words shape-changing like gods. *F*'s, *V*'s. Not that many *v*'s in English: virago, vertigo, voluptuous. Fewer *x*'s. Xerox. *X* equals *z*. Xylophone."

"Could have been xbra, for xample."

"Very good. Anyway—*v*, *x*. Think early Kim Novak."

"Kim Novak?"

"Movie actress. Blonde. *Vixen*. Female fox, short, quick

steps. Trot. Faster than a walk for horses. Fox-trot. And, we said as kids, 'Hot to trot': She Wants to Do It."

Another sip of scotch. "Also, unless I've recovered this memory, *Vixen* was a fifties magazine, lived in barbershops, under young male mattresses. Word evolving, it no longer meant shrewish but foxy. As in 'foxy lady!'"

"Am I foxy?"

"Yes, baby vixen. Baby she-fox."

"Shame on you."

"You heard a homonym? Shame on *you*." Another sip. "Awfully quick, English-as-a-second-language baby. Wordplay baby."

An older cousin, soon after his prostate surgery—and so, the writer gathered, at the end of his phallic adventure—told the writer that a middle-aged man seeing a young woman has to remember it's only a pause on his way to oblivion. For the young woman, he continued, the older man's an interlude on her way to Family, to Happy Ever After.

The writer's daughter. A step ahead of him while, always, professing jeopardy. It amuses the writer, but also he thinks she's wise. Why shouldn't she have it her way? He himself's gotten what he said he wanted more times than he cares to remember.

The writer bumps into a woman he dated in his early twenties. Once upon a time, she'd have given the world for him. And though she was ironic about everything not them—mocking the squares, the uglies!—now her irony includes what they were. How crazy he was, how crazy she was for knowing him. But, he thinks, she went on to some-one more crazy. And, since her current husband drove off the road, her chin's reconstructed, cast of her face quite different.

The writer goes home, takes out a picture of them years before. How lovely she was, how much affection she had to give. He should have treated her better, have let her go long before she left, but who could blame him for holding on?

The writer wonders. Is the hunger to recapture that youth—hers, his? For beauty possessed without aware-ness? Greed for a second chance, this time with hindsight, capacity to understand such grace.

His daughter's insistent—doesn't want to be with younger men. Not seasoned enough, too raw (or danger-ous—too much like herself, perhaps!). She does like flirting with them, however, calls them fish. But only flirts, she maintains. Loves the writer for all he's lived, would not have desired him before. She studies a photo of him at twenty-two, then one from the trip to the cabin. Places the photos side by side. "You were a prince back then," she tells him, "but now you're a king."

"Dear one, where in the world do you get these lines?"

She's undaunted. "I will want you when you're ninety."

The writer's sure he knows better. He'll be dead and gone long before, and she won't want to be around someone bedeviled by aging. Sex and death. People mock the phrase. Perhaps, the writer tells himself, perhaps it's more like Desire and Loss.

Urgent hunger to see each other is matched by impediments. One day, meeting her at the BART station after several weeks, he's struck by all the lies, evasions. This particular morning, as he pulls up and opens the car door, she seems quite ordinary, and nothing but trouble. What had come over him? Some kind of postsurgical spell?

Later, when her passion has once again ignited his, he strokes her hair. She draws him to her, wriggling. Baby salmon.

"Please," she says. "I love when you do that."

He continues to stroke her hair, for himself, for her. Asks, without any expectation of an answer, "Is this what all the fuss was about?" Remembers, for a flickering moment, his mercurial heart, the several times he's fallen, hard, out of love. At such moments, a real gift for repudiation.

Heart. Hard. Hard-hearted: not at all beyond his capacities.

. . .

Writing: blue-collar work, he'd told the cardiologist. And, during the hewing and drayage, book becoming coterminous with self.

"How's the book?" his daughter asks.

"I'm fine. And you?"

The stresses he's been cautioned about, sure, but how she's reawakened his love of story! Life savored in the retelling. And, no surprise, she wants to read the project he's working on.

"My models, sex, and death book? You're writing fiction. What have I seen of it?"

"I'm not there yet. Right now I'm reading Katherine Mansfield. Her beautiful use of detail. It's inspiring, she has a lot to teach me."

"But what's this fiction about?"

"I could be writing the story of a woman in love with her father."

"Write about us if you want. In any case, how does your story come out?"

"I don't know."

"A happy ending?"

"It will be like life."

"Oh, tragedy. More lieder." They laugh.

"But back to my question," she says. "What about your models, sex, and death project?"

"When it's done, dear one. Which will be a while."

"Just tell me this, do I get kissed in your book?"

"Maybe. If you're good."

Long since, the writer's used to being read. Solitary labor, and then, poof—others. The ever-strange mix of autonomy and dependence. He imagines another bumper sticker: WRITERS KEEP SUBMITTING.

Like other women the writer's been close to, his daughter reads him in part through the lens of self-interest. Quotes chapter and verse, sure she's apprehended him as no one else has. Still, the writer notes, she makes no mention of a story of his that might be germane. Published two decades before, it's about a theatrical, intelligent woman who's unfaithful to her husband, always with high rhetoric about love.

As for what he has yet to create, his daughter insists she wants all his stories, certain he hasn't told what he was born to write. He cherishes her for this, but there's more than one tale he's not prepared to articulate, perhaps even to himself. Change? Moltings, betrayals. Bloodletting. Is this what art can justify, validate? Will his daughter be prepared to render, say, this story only the two of them know? When? To whom?

Because she admires Duras, after finishing *The Lover* he picks up *The War*. Duras's diary recounts how she nurses her husband when he returns from a German death camp, and then, finally certain he'll survive, explains that she's been seeing someone, anyway would have wanted a divorce.

"Read this," the writer tells his daughter. "Like him I haven't been able to eat for seventeen days. Like him I haven't slept for seventeen days, or at least that's what I think."

"Oh," she says, laughing. "Still worrying this point? My father, like any sensible child, I'm going to do as you do, not as you say."

One day, just before they make love, she sets her wedding ring on the night table. After that, whenever she arrives, the ring is there until she prepares to leave.

"More prop than promise now," she says one evening, working the diamond over the knuckle. Tears in those large blue eyes.

The promise of marriage. A woman the writer advised about her how-to book is a marriage counselor, which in her practice can mean trying to help people separate without destroying each other. Her husband of thirty years, a psychiatrist, is droll, unflappable.

Joining them for lunch, the writer has a question for the husband.

"What do you call it when a man can imagine himself as the woman he's with?"

"He can imagine himself as the woman he's with?"

"I mean, he wants for her what he'd want for himself. Or even more."

"What he'd want for himself, or even more. Anything else?"

"Well, the man knows he has the capacity to injure a woman when he feels his interests diverge from hers. Withholdings, acts of commission."

"Acts of commission?"

The writer is tiring of the echo. "I mean, negative acts."

"Okay. Negative acts. Go on."

"Anyway, he knows he wants not to do that to this woman. Actually, he wants for her what she wants, though this is, at least in degree, a new feeling for him. Clear?"

"Clear. So what's the question?"

The writer can't resist. "What's the question?"

"Right. What's the question?"

The writer gives it up. "Well, what do you call that?"

"What do I call that?"

"Yes. What do you call that?"

"Love." Pauses. "Love."

The writer's disappointed. "That's it? Even if to want what she wants isn't good for her or them? You know, spoils her, makes her monstrous. That's all still love?"

"Yup. That's what it is." The psychiatrist beams, turns to his wife. "Right, Honey?"

·  ·  ·

As if it might induce clarity, the writer makes a mental list. His daughter:

- doesn't much like children, though she adores cats, small dogs
- is afraid of Nature
- has no "sensible shoes"
- is a night owl, loves to dance, won't miss a party
- hates confrontation, to disappoint
- paints her toenails red
- is careful to frequently wash her hands
- eats with gusto (and takes large portions, often leaving much on her plate without compunction)
- is ticklish
- rides her bike on sidewalks only
- shrieks when she drops something or the bathwater's too hot, enjoys both the shriek and its effect on others
- is fervent, *ardent:* glowing with earnestness, zeal
- sleeps soundly, sleep of the just, like any lucky child
- dislikes being alone.

Alone. Writer, having sought out being on his own so many times, reading John Donne: "One might almost say, her body thought."

Really, lists or no, he can't recall anything like it. Her.

# SUBJECT/OBJECT

N ew color prints.

- Of the yellow roses she brings, vase on kitchen table.
- She kneels on the bed, on her forearms, black halter top revealing the sphere of her breasts as she looks at the camera, at the writer.
- A shot of his chest, whorls of hair ever more dense. She loves that hair, she says, though such unsolicited proliferation makes him uneasy. Nothing can stop it, he thinks, or any other function of the passage of time.
- Over his down jacket, his father's red silk scarf with paisley print. The writer's face seems to him thin, drawn, eyelids more pronounced. And that scar on his

chin, so many years later, still so very visible. Interrogated by more than one lover. Irresistible, stories told about the scar in response to such earnest inquiry. Which one was true?

His face. Back slightly, giving him an ironic expression. But what is it that he knows? He's reminded of a picture of his mother taken when she's nearly seventy. Her chin forward, up. Air of bemusement, remove. Amiable, but *froideur*. As if she knows what the person behind the camera does not: game's over. That this moment is one more of life's poses. Or, though she's too courteous to ask, what does the photographer think a photo preserves? Saves one from?

She's just back from a conference, delivered a paper on Rodin and Rilke, Akhmatova and Modigliani. Aspects of her dissertation's "interrogation of intersections between visual and verbal." (Akhmatova posed for Modigliani, she explains to the writer.) It also appears she's going to do well in the upcoming job market, meaning she and her husband will probably leave town.

In a photograph taken at the conference, she's flanked by males: two job seekers to one side, professor on the other. Men in jacket and tie. Each of the four, name tag pinned, faces the camera. The professor's left hand, as if mentoring, clasps his right. Having chosen a gray tweed jacket over black blouse, lipstick an intense red, she has her hair up, fingers interlaced. Baby decorous.

To celebrate her job prospects, he brings her to a restaurant by the bay. Polynesian Pop: palm trees, thatched roof. Mélange of intentional bad taste, the once exotic, the bogus exotic, the retro. So much that's ersatz, reminding the writer how complex he's found the South Pacific in his years of wandering. She, meanwhile, takes it all in, pleased by her looking, as if the restaurant's a kind of museum, the nearby drunk salesmen on cell phones a living diorama.

The writer stops the waiter.

"Will you take a picture of my daughter and me?" She laughs: first time either of them has used the word in public.

As the waiter holds the camera, she leans the side of her head against the writer's shoulder, is wearing a lavender sweater. His sunglasses are up on his forehead, his hands clasped, one of hers holding them. Tapa cloth, carved god, surf photos behind.

Click. Flash. "My daughter thanks you," the writer tells the waiter.

. . .

His mother's hair. "Only your hairdresser knows for sure," went the Clairol ads of the sixties. His mother has a dressmaker, who makes the floor-length gowns for her lieder recitals, but no hairdresser. Her hair: never changed, cut, colored, tinted. Not negotiable. Like his father's mustache, and, later, the writer's. Commitment to one chosen transformation of self.

Childhood, again passing through the walnut doors into his parents' bedroom and study. Yet another morning after the household gets rolling. His parents' double bed not quite finished being made, white chenille spread waiting on chaise longue. His mother's writing desk in the alcove. His father's closet door open, line of charcoal suits, many red/dark red/red-black ties draped over the wooden bar— practical solution to his father's color blindness—and pairs of polished black shoes, shoe trees within. The fragrance of aftershave.

In the morning, everyone having had breakfast, his mother is back upstairs, standing in dressing gown in front of the full-length wall mirrors, or in front of the bathroom mirror, combing her hair. Down, down to her waist, stroke after stroke. (She can sit on her hair, his sister reminds him.) So much care for something merely ornamental. Though it does not seem ornamental: simply hers; her.

As always, his mother starts to braid. Deft, the fingers,

separating thick flow into three clusters, twining a single plait, an elastic to seal the ends, then a turning, her left to her right, hair pins fixing coil in place. Order, control—and she has so much self-control, imposes so much order on the household—just after, despite, so inviting a torrent of freedom, plentitude.

There's a poem his mother writes in her forties, narrator describing a teenager's yearning. Young woman who lets down her hair, gives away freely of her house, extends a hand "to the climber coming in over the sill."

The writer's mother is hospitalized at seventy-three, "short-term" becoming months. Nothing unusual: one way things end. Her ever-expanding hospital stay, surprising only to her grown children, terminates in yet another complication, coma, and death. Their mother's hair bespeaks what's gone wrong. Turns white, belatedly, overnight. As if color too had been susceptible to will.

In the hospital, her hair is down except when one of the writer's sisters decides to put it up. Restoring their mother somewhat to what she's been to herself, to them, but of course infantilizing her in the doing. Her hair, thus, often unkempt, betraying six decades' attentive practice. Making her look like . . . someone else.

Spending the night, his daughter wears a pair of the writer's black cotton pants, torso and feet bare. Stands, back to him, dividing her long brown hair—she too can sit on hers—into, what do you know, three clusters.

"Take one of the outside sections," she explains, "and

put it across into the middle. Now take the new outside one, place it in the middle." He's struck dumb, so much welling up from memory, but she's waiting. Continues to like him to help, though he prefers just watching. As he did as a child. Incredibly quick fingers; her shoulder blades, long neck, long arms, breasts seen from behind and to the side. Her pleasure letting the hair cascade onto his chest as she straddles him, just after that final movement of approach, startlingly fast. Predator accelerating, blur of intentionality, to beloved kill.

There's that first time at the bay, his head in her lap, when she unpinned her hair. No word of explanation. Her long hair not cut for years. She seems to savor the tension between hair up, hair down. Between, say, maturity and youth, control and sensuality, modesty and display.

("In the other life," she tells the writer, "my hair is almost never down." This, however, proves inaccurate: leafing through photos she gives him, he's unhappy to see she's misremembered.)

The next morning, she's in the bathroom, naked at the mirror except for her black high heels, about to plait her hair. Arms up and behind, elbows out, breasts lifted. Hair dropping well below her waist. The writer's eyes, gorging, drawn down with it.

. . .

More than once, her mouth is there, ravenous, licking, striving, sucking, right at the tip, as if at the breast. He holds that coiled mass of hair in his left hand, tight, at the roots, precluding her from more. Sets the limit simply . . . for the pleasure of setting a limit.

"Yes?" he asks.

"Yes, I like to submit." When she chooses, of course. "Oh my love, please don't stop." How he savors the "please." Which, he's surprised to realize, she finds difficult to say, like a teenager.

Once, in her from behind, her long arms spread like wings, he tries to extort a "please." But she won't be more than willingly coerced.

"I never do anything against my will," she tells him.

This, though, being carried farther from the heart of her marriage, astride him one day she begins to strike at his chest with her fists. Hard. And, later, well aware of what she's not giving him, saying, "Please hurt me. Please."

He tells his daughter her love of language and her clothing remind him of his mother. And there is something early '50s about her, makeup and (often) conservative demeanor suggesting another time, albeit with spin. A summer dress his daughter wears: for a moment the writer is back in Cambridge, age ten, at the Blacksmith Shop, having pastry, the day humid, slow, chestnut trees providing opulently leafy shade.

Later, they again examine the possibility they'd dismissed—that his daughter is in fact his mother. "I think not," he says, "but yours is the body I know second best."

A connection is there, some extraordinary conduit from earliest yearning to this union now. His daughter feels no threat. Still, when she chides him, there's risk: "You remind me unfavorably of my mother." A recalcitrant child, he received enough correction to last a lifetime. Enough competing for love, of strong, purposive people. His mother a propagandist for her marriage, for her extraordinarily good husband. Also, not surprisingly, propagandist against her children's desires except as they coincided with her sense of what desire should be.

It was not his mother's task, she hardly could have strived to make it clear, say, that her love for their father was her deepest love. Or that children were a strenuous ambiguity for her, a responsibility best expressed through caring discipline.

What remains emerges as story. Partial truths, quasi-truth. "My mother never just admitted that my father was the one for her," the writer hears himself say to his daughter one day in bed, and again they laugh.

Another time, the writer decides he wants his daughter

to listen to a recording of his mother in performance. He forgets he has not heard his mother's voice in the fifteen years since she died. Inserts the tape, presses PLAY. And there she is, as if never gone. There's no stopping: he begins to cry.

That melting, as they call it. Often, resting after she's come another time, they surface from such unintended concentration. Pure present: mouths fastened for, who knows, five minutes, ten? Someone's tongue probing someone's inner cheek, sucking lower lip. Merging; impelled by, feeding on, itself.

Bewitched. Drifting, dreaming; one flesh. But, oops: hand on, under, around. In her once again.

She licks here, cradles there, looks up. "Isn't it wonderful being a man?"

And surely she finds it wonderful to be a woman. "Something unimportant happened," she tells him in their first days together, and the phrase becomes an ongoing joke. "Something unimportant."

"My daughter, you're outnumbering me, maybe thirty to one."

"Merely coming from behind, so to speak. All those women you've loved."

"I think you just surpassed me. And I'm a lot older.

Also, you're seeing two people. I'm seeing just one. Baby Casanova."

She studies him thoughtfully. "I've never given myself like this before. Ever."

"Poor baby hyperbole. Now you've gone and committed another overstatement." Making allowance for heat of moment, weakness of memory, revisionism.

"Oh, I wish it were." And, in her marvelously exaggerated way, or so it seems to him, starts to weep.

She'd never used sexually explicit language. That "take me," the first time. Her verbal reticence only heightening the sense of violation.

Months pass before she can say the words he uses, and then only as if in quotes. Until, finally, they're hers, for the pleasure of them both hearing her say them. Surprisingly, the words continue to gratify.

"I love your vulva," he tells her one day. He'd been "sucking her dry," as she puts it. Has been considering it closely. Hands-on investigation. This is long after she informed him, their first day, that she required "penetration." Determined then to remind him she had a husband. That people thought they were newlyweds still, "like Romeo and Juliet."

"Romeo and Juliet were fourteen or fifteen. And died."

She ignored him. Was conveying she knew what she liked. "I prefer making love in the morning." And, "I love making love when it's snowing." Putting Casanova in his place. Or perhaps, he thought, she was just young. And clueless.

Nothing stays the same. Now she helps him take the picture: spreads her legs, two quite different hands pulling open this side, the other. One of his hands out of the shot cupping camera; her forefinger depressing shutter. Circle of darker skin below, around what they call, grinning at the euphemism, her "other passage," sunbeams radiating out from center.

"My hand's a portcullis," he says, before looking up the word with her. Portcullis: grating that slides in grooves at the sides of a castle gateway, let down to prevent entry. Actually, his hand is less safeguard than intruder. "How tight, how strong," he tells her. "Now this is the ring I want." She flexes as he probes, proud of the flexing. Suddenly shrieking once again.

"That's a first," she tells him, perhaps informing out of a sense of fair play, also taking note of it herself. Later, she says, as if relating an unexpected fact to herself and obliged to disclose it, "You've given me a much closer relationship with my sexuality." Laughing, but, it seems, meaning it.

And the pictures. She holds the Polaroid, is herself in the photo only below the waist. There he is, eyes closed, nose and mouth obscured by pubic hair merging with mustache, right hand above pubic bone, pulling, pulling.

In another shot she takes—artist; fount—he has a hand on each of her hips. Her mound lifts, rises, his head between thighs. Eyes closed, he's . . . meditating? Forehead veins bulging. And despite the burden of art—flash of bulb, whir as camera ejects image—she's in as well as outside of the moment.

One last shot. He's staring up at her, eyes glazed, as if from alcohol, exhaustion. Her left hand on his head, steadying, encouraging. "I'm completely destroyed," she often says, laughing, after they make love. Which is how he now looks. Completely destroyed.

She stands in the bedroom, hair up, neck exposed. Naked, looking down as if lost in thought. Right breast in profile, nipple hard. Wrists tied behind with cord of red velour. He'd gone to a fabric store, chosen from among hundreds of spools. Salesperson, a young woman, cheerful, supportive.

His daughter, bound. What's she thinking? How she ever got into such insanity? Or, perhaps, asking herself again, as she once did out loud, "What is this?"

Seeing her there, the writer says, "Oh, my tufted tit-mouse."

"Untie me, please. I want to look it up."

Unfettered by language: tufted titmouse. No mouse at all—a bird. But that tuft. Arrowhead, pointing. He wants to shave her, sets out his razors—electric, hand. Brushes. Comb. More than once she says no, though between them the yeses are accumulating. Becoming inexorable.

Both of them are hysterical with laughter when he finally takes scissors in hand—"Show me mercy," she says—and clips several hairs, and those just near the ends. Which he then puts in his mouth. And swallows.

"Communion," he hears himself offer, as if he'd had a plan.

Several days later, she brings him a weekly newspaper, sex columnist addressing the subject of pubic hair. This is proving typical of his daughter: reluctant, then pushing them on. As if, he tells himself, as if she senses she may not pass this way again.

"What do you think," she asks, "about what the journalist terms 'the pedophilia aspect of shaven pudenda'?"

"So much alliteration. And what are pudenda, anyway?"

"Please respond to the question."

"Pederasty? Deemed nasty. Philately? She left her stamp on me. All right, all right. Pedophilia. Guilty. Especially deplorable when combined with incest."

"But what else about shaving me there?"

He holds the article, reads, "Genitals darken and engorge with blood during arousal." Looks over at her, eyes twinkling. "Sounds right."

"It's the word *engorge* that stirs me," she replies.

"Me too, dear one. I'm even stirred by the verb *stir.*"

Tropes of the gods' sexual affairs with nymphs or mortals. Love at first sight followed by refusal, flight, pursuit. And metamorphosis—seducers and maidens disguised, or transforming punishment imposed by a jealous divinity.

"My Zeus," his daughter says again. "How relentless you are." Now, as Ovid might put it, the kindler burns.

Odd, the fate of images. Early on, the writer shows her a postcard he loves. Poseidon, bronze statue recovered from the sea in the 1920s. Face of the naked god arrogant, serene. Schematic curls gathered, plaited. Right arm poised to strike with the trident he must have been holding, horizontal left arm as counterbalance.

For the writer, this image is from years before. Women ago. Athens, the National Museum. Poseidon Earthshaker: the writer was in Greece, swimming miles a day in the truly wine-dark Aegean, in his element. *Thalassa.* And the Pleiades. Sunrises, moonrises. Poseidon Earthshaker: one day the writer nearly drowned.

Greek art. Several pictures they take in the mirror while

making love are as if from a kylix. Writer behind, hands on her hips, penetrating. Segment of shaft visible, buttocks up high to receive, breasts crushed against blanket as she looks toward the camera. Crying out, "Oh, god, please don't stop."

Gods. Her story of the day she sees a card of the Poseidon statue at a girlfriend's house. "Yes," she tells her friend, "I know him."

# THIS TIDE OF WOMEN

She and her husband keep her camera handy, document their marriage. Several times, she gives the writer a print from "that life," perhaps to remind him it exists, to insist she cannot pay the price of giving it up.

One black-and-white photo: just after they've left a charity ball. It's late, sidewalk empty, sole car approaching. Urban forlorn, row of newspaper racks, shops dark. Lone female figure, shot from behind, moving away from the camera. The gown's bare shoulders and back; spike heels.

Always, in photographs, what can't be seen. In this case, that the woman in the gown and the writer spoke that morning. That, despite having to get ready for the dance, she decided to come over, running toward him as he stood waiting outside the cottage.

"Did we just make killer love?" she asked as she left, savoring the idiom.

Weeks later, she tells the writer that this photo is one of her husband's favorites. That he's had it enlarged, framed.

Writer waiting to hear from her, reading. A psychologist's view of life as a shuttling "back and forth between the solitary state and dyads, dyads and triangles, triangles and the solitary state, never finding [the] preferred state of rest."

"Is our communion only erotic?" Pay phone, three thousand miles away, she asks. Teases? Might better ask herself. On a business trip with her husband. The writer remembers being seventeen, the mandatory lies, half-truths, self-deceptions, assurances. "Only erotic." After she hangs up, he tells himself. Such faint praise could bring one of Dionysius's madwomen running to tear off head, arms, legs. What seems to him her extraordinary sexual intelligence. As if there's a sign on the highway of their passion: EROS AT WORK. VENUS UTILITY COMPANY.

On her return from Boston, she brings him a picture from South Station, waiting for a train, her long hair down. Looking anxious, coming up with an excuse to find a pay phone to ask a question across the country.

"This picture was taken for you," she says.

"You mean, 'I had this picture taken for you by my husband.'"

Other men's wives. Early on, the writer concluded that one should be "in love" to sleep with a friend's girlfriend or wife. When he was in his twenties, a friend regularly found bedmates in the gene pool of women in their circle. The writer noted the disruption of such betrayals, had his own, different, credo but refrained from passing judgment. Without having thought it through, he also believed love is blind, and unstoppable.

His not-yet-daughter. When, soon after they met, she invited the writer first to a party she and her husband were giving, then to the movies with them, he declined. The writer was drawn to her. If he was introduced to her husband, or, worse, liked him, he'd have to try to avoid being more attracted to her.

It's only later the writer explains this. She responds by explaining how surprised she was he kept saying no. Reminding him of an evening they bumped into each other at a café, both hesitating on the sidewalk before saying good night.

"Why didn't you kiss me as we stood there?" she says.

"You should have kissed *me.*"

"I couldn't. I wanted to, but I was married."

Was.

Is.

Ground rules. Never does she even imply criticism of her husband, is quick with praise. Not lawyer but brilliant lawyer, dedicated to the disenfranchised. Has not failed her in any way, cannot live without her. Has loved only her. Sees her as his universe. Needs her protection.

"How can I do this to him?" she asks. Still, nothing's to diminish the marriage: "It's essential to my nature." Also, "I could never hurt him."

The writer must understand. More, he must be jealous; otherwise, they're not in love, cannot see each other. She won't change her life, but is determined to be true to her need to know the writer, take care of him, learn what he has to teach her. But also, she wants to take possession, has, as it turns out, only one emotional gear.

"I hate compromise," she tells him. This in addition to, "If he ever finds out, I'll never see you again."

"Just don't sell us out," the writer says. Certain she will, if necessary.

As weeks pass, the writer wonders how she imagines she'll remain unaltered. But she seems to have successfully divided her life, two worlds separate, each operating on its own terms.

Psychologists say that in one aspect love is rivalrous—a desire to supplant or diminish competitors. Initially, however, their stolen nights together, the writer reminds her to call home as scheduled. To save her from herself. Not, since she says it's vital to her, to jeopardize her marriage. And why humiliate her husband? Further, perhaps, not to take on the burden of her, now that the writer's again used to being on his own. His splendid isolation, she calls it, admiringly, ironically. But as time passes, by the terms of a scenario plausible to the writer, they're sheltering her husband until she's ready to separate in what the writer imagines to be the right way. As the writer would want to be left? Still, the writer expects she'll—inadvertently, half inadvertently—make a mistake and it will all unravel. In the meantime, occasionally they walk around town as if invisible. As if she's determined to be seen. "To be found out in order to be stopped from going further," she suggests.

She shows him another photo. At her desk at home, deep blue dressing gown, hair down, working on a manuscript—text of a speech her husband's to deliver. Pen in hand, bookcases teeming. What she and her husband have created between them. She shows him the photo, the writer thinks, to ask him to spare it.

Three things she said one day:

- "I've promised my life to someone else."
- "I wish I had two lives."
- "Where you are is my home."

"Home away from home," he replies.

. . .

I want to be the best listener you've ever had," she says. Baby collector: "I want the stories you've never told." And, "I'm going to be your Muse."

That one emotional gear. Jealous. Of past, present, future. Of any woman he's been with, might be with. Fear of betrayal; anger at having been excluded from past relationships. She says, more than once, that if they're ever together she'll call "all the women," tell them to forget having known him. She means it, even though because she's so very married they'll never be together. Also, same proviso, she'll get his house keys, e-mail code, phone access number. She's just short of demanding them as it is.

She's jealous of his T-shirt: closer to his nipples than she is when she's away. "I'm jealous of my nipples, too," she says, laughing, when, it suddenly seems, he's paid them too much attention.

"I've never felt jealousy before," she tells him, and he believes her. She knew what she was doing when she chose her husband.

"I want to be the only one who thinks you're beautiful," she says, right after explaining that she'd like to show him off to others. "If people really see us as a couple, they'll be envious."

Her keen sense of the presence of rivals is a form of flattery—women find him irresistible. How can the writer deny it! Art, transformation. Her appetites are enormous, operatic, and so her imaginings, fears.

The engine of her desire. "It's really not jealousy," she says, trying to clarify. Justify. "It's a craving for possession." She marks the cottage. Perfume in his bathrobe. Gift of new sheets, of course. Shirts. Pearl earring in the corner behind the dresser. Panties in the drawer with his underwear.

As for the fact she's still making love with her husband?

"Almost never now. But what does it matter? I only give myself to you."

The writer shakes his head, grudgingly admires the aplomb. The casuistry.

"You don't think my argument's sincere?" She's grinning. And then, as if to placate him, and/or to hear the sound of herself saying such words, adds, "I'd never been properly fucked before." "Fucked" still in quotes.

One day, when she says again she's glad the writer's not younger, he asks if she doesn't believe the women he's known helped make him who he is.

"No."

"I'm a machine. They kept the parts from getting rusty."

They laugh, but the women he's loved—and not loved, who loved or didn't love him—shaped, often were, his life. Their affection giving him the sure center from which he could explore even the dark side of love's moon. Years of loyalty, the domestic. The quotidian, the almost trivial:

recipe for the garlic linguine his daughter devours, from a dancer in Paris ten years before; the gel, first demonstrated for him by a painter he dated, lubricant she learned of from . . . her fiancé. O Schnitzlerian chain of being! But, his daughter tells him, "No." Adds, thoughtfully, "I'm really only built for first love."

Another time, she says, "I want to write your biography someday."

"I can guess how it will begin. 'Few people realize that my father was a sexual innocent when we first met.'"

Biography. They read a life of Tolstoy, libertine giving a virgin bride his journals their wedding night. Tolstoy was wrong, the writer argues: this record of dissipations caught only a fraction of his life's truths. But now it became his wife's story to torment them both with. The past as formula, reduced again after Tolstoy had reduced it to the page.

His daughter begs to differ. "My father, Tolstoy must have wanted to be known in this way."

"If so, he surely lived to regret it."

The writer and his past. Though she loves his books, she'd like to "tear out" offending anecdotes, dedications. All that breaks her heart. His many lives: is there anything not long since given away?

"You haven't changed too much, my love, wouldn't you agree?" Citing bathtub, cottage, fish pier.

Conceding the continuities, the writer can't abide her reading his fiction as autobiography. The stories cost too much. Work that wrote them and emotions mined, transmuted. As for the women he's loved, he has his formulae; just to get along has done his own redacting. He can, nonetheless, evoke more complex truths, doesn't want anyone doing violence to them. Also feels protective of the women who cared for him, even if he was less kind than he should have been.

So: his daughter has no right to these stories. Or to the others: his unstated, unorganized, thus-far-unfinished life with the women who preceded her.

His daughter's more than disappointed, wants his "history," despite so much of him already there to read.

"My thoughts are my own," the writer retorts. "You have too much at stake. Some of what's true, I'll take to the grave with me."

Take to the grave. Did I really just say that? the writer wonders.

Othello's war stories. Desdemona's "greedy ear." What the writer's daughter wants, does not want, to hear. To possess by knowing. But also, what excites, even if it repels. As if in asking to hear such stories she's admitting, gaining, a new part of her sexual self. His daughter presses him for a story about a young woman he once dated. "Was she a virgin?" Wants to know more, but then can't take the how. Stops him. Weeps.

"I'm going to get my own virgin."

"But you're married."

"That's not the point. You've outnumbered me. By a factor of thousands."

"Hundreds."

The writer winces, remembers a man who used to talk about his lovers. Not surprisingly, his young wife concluded such variety was to be experienced, didn't mind establishing parity.

"But you're already the baby Casanovita, seeing two men."

"I'm in love with two men," she says emphatically, "not 'seeing them.'"

Who she loves, who he sees. She calls the next morning. "Did I wake you?"

"No. Just cleaning up after the concubines."

"Plural? How many?"

"Six. What a mess. They never pick up after themselves. Like teenagers. I'm worn out."

"Too much lovemaking?"

"No. I only made love to two of them. The other four stayed up all night talking. I barely slept a wink."

"Poor Zeus."

*Concubines.* The word suits his reluctance to be explicit about who he's seeing—or not—when she's with her husband. But also, appropriate to her desire to relegate to secondary status anyone he might be with. Consonant too with her sense that he has women he could be with. Finally, *concubine* as threat but also funny, because it's archaic and because . . . there are none.

"You know," he tells her, "if there are concubines, they'll be people. Names, faces, biographies. Just like us. Like your husband."

She's silent. Married, she knows when it's not worth a fight.

Baby Odysseus? Sartorial problem. Finally returning home, Odysseus disguises himself as a beggar. Baby-baby wouldn't want that, would she? But, as she's joked, like Odysseus she's trickster, storyteller. As the writer surely was at her age. In part, because she hates confrontation. Ongoing lie to her aunt. Incessant deception of her husband. And, though she insists she tells the writer everything, lies of omission.

Early on, when she and the writer are still just talking, the word *transparency* comes up. The gist: no point lying to each other. One of their first days together, she tells him she made love to her husband after she and the writer separated the previous time. But as their bond grows, as she's afraid of losing what the two of them share, the truth gets harder to express.

Truth. Early on, she tells him she's five nine, but then starts laughing. Five eight and a half, actually.

"Say you're sorry."

"I don't enjoy apologizing."

"You have to."

"All right. Sorry."

"Sorry? You really are twelve."

"Why?"

"Kids get around an apology by avoiding the pronoun. So, tell your father, dear one, who's sorry?"

"I'm sorry."

"Good baby."

"Child abuser." She brightens. "Now you tell me, have you ever lied to me?"

"Oh, very clever."

"Well, have you?"

"Not yet," he lies. "But I may sometime soon."

"Say you will be sorry."

"I will be sorry? Okay, dear one, I will be sorry." Thinking how little she knows him. And how clever she is. "You're quick," he adds, and means it.

To mean it. Much of what she says is that extraordinary overstatement. "I'm yours." "I can't live without you." But, amazed by how soon she can return to her other life, he asks what the words signify.

"I'm being honest at the time, when I say them."

He laughs. God, he finds it appealing, the way she throws herself on his mercy.

"As your father, I applaud your strategy."

"You're the only one who knows everything about me."

"Perhaps I know more than most people. Let's leave it at that."

When she meets her husband-to-be she's seventeen. Just arrived here. He's older, a family friend, her first lover. She makes no promise to be faithful, has turned down many suitors. Makes him wait. Meets a married film-maker. Is soon seeing both men. Inevitably, her husband-to-be finds out she's drawn to someone else. In the ensuing craziness, both men "weeping," witnessing the suffering of her husband-to-be—she's his first love—she resolves to marry him.

In her narrative to her husband-to-be, not surprisingly, she fails to mention that she and the filmmaker are lovers. Why state the almost obvious? She remembers, however: how many times they slept together—dates, places. Recorded on a tape loop in her memory. Destroys the photographs of them. Savors such eradication in favor of her husband.

"There was nothing more I wanted from the filmmaker. I'd responded to what was between us. He was the one who wept."

The writer has his own tape loop, going back to their

first conversations. "Is the filmmaker the one who told you life's not a book?"

"Very good. Yes."

"So you'll destroy my letters, photos of us? As it is, you've got them hidden, packed away."

"You're the love of my life." Then, as if answering the unspoken question, she says, "I just can't unlove someone, that's all."

Threnody," he tells her. "Casanova's threnody." She looks it up.

"Song of lamentation, funeral song, dirge."

"Good baby. How about bereft?"

"Past tense of bereave," she says. "Deprived, left sad and lonely."

"And bereave?"

"To rob, as of life, or hope."

"Poor baby, the maybe-baby, the cry-baby baby."

"Poor Casanova."

Weekends are when he doesn't see her, or, generally, hear from her: she's with her husband. Weekends, he's surprised to find, become interminable. Surprised, because he's always liked time alone. Because he knew she was married. Still, if asked, he'd say, "The separations are killing me." So to speak.

Flowers. Young Hal and the writer laughed that day on their walking meditation, but Hal's spiritual practice is about inner quiet. Began in fear, when, mesmerized, he hung around the gangstas in high school, realized he might get himself beaten, shot. Met an ex-con who'd saved himself in prison by meditating.

Nonattachment. The writer, heart repaired, still alive; his daughter's departures, disappearances. The mind grinds. To rant, to remonstrate. Exclusions, tantalizations. Anger, reproach, powerlessness. Casanova loses it. Half empty? Half full? Writer, trying to write his way out of it. A letter, sent to her aunt's:

> Dear one:
>
> You may remember, arms extended above your beautiful hair, bathrobe sash turned twice around your wrists, nothing you couldn't undo. Or my leather belt. Baby-baby. I coiled the belt round my hand, touched your nipples, brushed you there. You were wet, left your mark. I didn't know where I was going. Your yes did it all. The same when you hit me or I hit you while we were making love—for the harm it would do, for what might have to be acknowledged. How could you not have waited? How could you have made me wait? How can you imagine you can leave? How could you think it wouldn't change you, change everything?
>
> Baby monster. You may remember the bathtub,

black bamboo out the window. Neighbor fixing, grinding. Polaroids, that defiant yes. Your beautiful breasts. So in the tub I said it was more difficult than you might think, meaning want was in the way of want, meaning your yes was taking me where I'd never been, as you put it, before.

Not long ago, I cried to hear my mother's voice. You were there. Goading me for more stories. Now you ask, "Do you know what you're doing?" And just today you said, "I've never really known passion before." And, you said, "Desire begins with you and ends with you."

She loves to work, will wrap up her Ph.D. in record time. Is also built for not-work: another film to see; oh, those crab cakes in New York. She's prone, nonetheless, to the eros of unhappiness. More than once, the writer thinks of Heine's poems in the lieder cycles. "I wept in my dream; I dreamt you were lying in your grave . . . I wept in my dream; I dreamt you were leaving me."

"You made me weep," his daughter says; "I almost wept." Moved to tears, and by them. Crying: as no, as yes. Voluptuous, but also conveying the tearful imperative of the child. Cathartic, manipulative, unintended, tyrannical tears. She also sometimes weeps when she comes. "This is love," she's shouting. Weeping.

"You would never put up with me," she tells him. "I'm too needy for you."

The writer wonders, what could he put up with? Roaming no more, he feels, this Casanova. At the café at six in the morning, he's sobered to see only single men in middle age, old age.

Gone again, she phones long distance, argues her rhetoric is heartfelt. "Words are actions." She now frequently says "I love you," but he's angry; she's gone.

"Anger is a form of crying," he tells her.

"So, are you leaving me?"

"I'm not done with you yet," he hears himself reply.

Back from his morning cappuccino at the café, the writer scans the paper: Men with depression are "2.34 times more likely to die of heart disease than non-depressed men." The linkage seems to be depression/stress/constricted blood vessels/blocked arteries. His daughter still asleep, the writer broods.

She yawns. "My father. Where's my mocha?"

"No mocha today."

"Oh." She stretches, looks at him appraisingly. "Am I still your only daughter?"

"No."

"And your baby?"

"No. I don't like you anymore."

She laughs. "You sound five years old."

"I don't like you anymore."

"Really?"

"You're too old for me."

Tears come to her eyes. "Please don't say that. Take it back."

There's a silence, as both regroup. As if waiting to see what other damage will be inflicted.

"You're in academia."

"Yes."

"You know, I've never liked it when academics use *privilege* as a verb."

"And?"

"Now I'm going to use it as a verb."

She nods.

"I no longer privilege your marriage."

Is there a rival?" she asks plaintively. "Is there anything I should know?"

He's silent.

"What's on your mind?"

"Baby Carmen," he finally replies.

"Why?"

"I just remembered. The video you gave me that day at the cottage. Men going crazy with jealousy."

"What about it?"

"Two men competing before you married, and, after a spell of dedicated monogamy, here you are again. Baby Carmen. Afraid I'll be just like her."

"My father. I don't like how you're connecting the dots. You're more gallant than that."

Was, he thinks. Never was, he thinks, remembering how little he likes being dependent. Remembering some of the scores he's kept. Settled.

Making the case against her. No problem. Begin with the petty. For instance, she's always late. Calling her husband or aunt to say she'll be late. Greed in the form of overbooking? Lack of fear? Desire to play the diva? Trust that nothing she does will cause her to lose the love of others?

"Not fair," she says, when he shares this speculation with her.

"Why not, pray tell?"

"It's because of us, of you. Like the lying."

The writer thinks it over, admits the at least partial merit of her point. As usual, she's about to go upstairs to use the phone in private.

"You're going to call home and your aunt?"

"Just my aunt. I'm not going to call home."

"You mean, you already did."

She laughs. "My father is too good a liar to lie to."

"Maybe. Are you going to continue to try to lie to me?"

"I'll let you know if I do."

"No. Tell me before."

"Be aware, I'm about to lie. . . ?"

"Yes, that's my daughter," he says. "Wicked, like me."
Setting aside the case against her, at least for the moment.

A nother letter from the writer sent to her aunt's:

> Dear one: You've stayed away, you've withheld,
> you owe me, so—I will cheat, steal, misuse, abuse,
> traduce, confuse you.
>
> "I'll be defenseless," you say, and we both laugh.
>
> But I will ransack, vandalize, pillage, despoil you.
>
> "Whatever you want," you respond.
>
> But baby, despoil is not to spoil.
>
> You say, "I will write my will before I see you, do
> my laundry, pay off my credit cards. I will be yours,
> that I know for sure."
>
> Not enough: I tell you again, I'm not a good per-
> son, or, only intermittently. When I can't help it. Not
> most of the time. No.
>
> You say, "You might 'fuck up' my life." "I'm wait-
> ing to be woken up by you, like Sleeping Beauty."

It pleases me to get even. How I see it. You come in the door, we give you a bath, like before, like always. You're kissing me. Sucking my lower lip, panting. Moaning. The way you do.

I wash your breasts, then my hands go below. Towel falls. We don't quite get you dry. Bedroom: oh, am I prepared. Red velour cord round each ankle and wrist, on to leg of bed. I take you in my mouth. You keep pulling at me to come up, in. Look. On your back, spread wide. I move a pillow, you lift. In my mouth again. Your sounds, sounds.

Finally I stop, leaving you there to think it over. Will he return? Why did he go? He really is crazy, you'll be saying to yourself, pulling at the cords. This isn't funny. But there I am again, "Hi, baby, I'm back." "Will you be gentle?" you asked today. Yes, dear one, I promise. All my violence will be gentle.

Laughing, you say, "Whatever you want," and, "You know I'm yours."

Mine for now, you mean.

But damned if I don't again consent to the terms implied. Still, despite this yes, I really don't know how far I'll go. Dear one, it's my nature, my fate, I'll stand beside the bed, and you'll be wondering—tied down, open so very wide—you'll be wondering where it all begins and ends and I'll be doing the numbers. *Take you?* Calculating, reckoning just how much I'll take from you. And why.

. . .

You won't believe what happened when I got home," she says. "My husband was reading *Anna Karenina*. He'd reached the scene where the count watches Anna flirting with Vronsky. He told me how lucky he was, that I'd never made him jealous. Uneasy, but not jealous. He said I was very trustworthy. For years, of course, he's had reason to think so."

"Yes."

"Then he said that if I got a fellowship to go abroad, he'd come with me. 'I don't care where I am with you,' he told me. 'You're my only country.'"

"Yes."

"Later, I argued with him about bills. About nothing. He just laughed, said I'd apologize. Then I did. But I can't do this. He's a good person. It's not right."

"No."

They're silent for several moments. "Want to hear a hard truth?" she asks.

"Not really."

"My father, the more you and I are together, the more I feel I owe him. What do you think about that?"

"What do I think?"

"Yes."

"Sounds plausible," the writer replies, more sympathetic to such emotional logic than he cares to be.

# THE BEHOLDER'S EYE

She calls. "I love to see you in my mouth in the mirror. I want to stroke you, lick you everywhere. I'll be all over you."

"You won't. Your tongue will get tired."

"Ssssh, my father. I'm going to study the Polaroids, come again and again."

"You took some of the Polaroids? Thief."

"Yes. I like seeing you, and us, and I like being in the photographs. I *love* being the object of desire."

Object of desire. The next day, they look at a photo taken a week before. He's on his back; she's astride, facing him. In the foreground, his chest, stomach, erect phallus, her open legs and pubic hair. Her two hands, closed, knuckles toward the camera, in the act of stroking. Snake charmer summoning, levitating. Or, as if she's trying to shinny up the gel-glistening phallus.

Another photo, very disturbing: her mouth gaping, eyes closed, head way back, hair tumbling down over shoulder and breast.

"She looks like she's been carried off by Zeus," she says. "Abducted. Ravished. I've never seen that woman before. I don't know her."

"I do, baby."

Well, yes, but the photo shows something the writer cannot claim to have seen in this way. "Throe" of passion—convulsion, agony, paroxysm. He's beheld her at such times, but never with the camera's distance, capacity to apprehend the moment for reconsideration. Being as he was, despite the impulse to record, in, overwhelmed by, the moment.

Hold yourself open for me," and she does.

"Pull back that beautiful hood."

"I love the word *hood*," she replies.

Later, his finger is in her, "thrumming," he says. Hand cupping. That finger, those fingers, here; thumb there. He feels his forearm's strength, is grateful, tells her so. Pushing, he notices the heel of her hand on her pubic hair.

"Dear one, we've lost one of your fingers."

"I'm trying to rescue it."

"Good baby. Please give me your other hand."

"Where?"

"Behind. On mine."

"Yes."

Over and over, this familiarity, play, as if the path's known, presumption of mutual desire, collaboration.

Desire. Once more it seems to him she wants things he'd want were he her, also that she wants what he wants, if only he will think to ask.

Grand gestures. One day, as they're about to leave the bedroom for yet another bath—"We're setting the world record for mandatory ablution," he tells her—she takes him by the hand, pulls him in front of the wall mirror. Slowly, back to him, arches forward. Reaching around, puts his shaft against that tighter passage. Says "Please," bending over, farther, farther, hair tumbling forward, until her fingertips touch the floor.

Again the bath.

"My Zeus. Did you like that?"

"Oh yes."

"Did you see me touch the floor?"

"Flexible baby. Screaming and weeping baby diva. Another first."

"Do you think we're one flesh?"

"Yes. Yes. One flesh. One mind, too."

Camera in hand, he's on his back, and she's astride, two hands cupping him below, about to guide him into her. Tip, engorged, approaching red O. Polaroid pictures strewn on the bed.

He's on his back. She's astride, facing his feet. In control of pace. Up slow, down very slow. Up, slower, again.

Later, studying the photograph together, they see section of shaft, lips open to swallow, tight circle above.

"Baby from behind," she says.

Viewfinder at eye, taking a picture as she comes once again.

"Stop," she moans, and he thinks he's let desire for the pictures intrude, overwhelm, replace.

"Stop? Why, baby?"

"Please, my father."

"But why?" Stalls, depresses the shutter.

"Oh my father, please. I need to see your face."

Don't get another mirror," she'd told him, in her frugal mode. But her head keeps turning toward it. "Oh, look at us." And, "Oh, look at you in me."

"You like the mirror? Baby narcissist."

She's unperturbed. "The mirror is read by Lesser as both 'instrument of self-regard' and 'self regarded.' My father, mirrors do invert, do transform life into the merely visible. But like art, they can offer new visions of the world. When we make love I see another self in the mirror. But also, I see another you. And another us. Yes?"

"Yes."

"You admit the complexity of my point?"

"Yes."

"Do you like how I invoked an authority?"

"Suasive. Rhetorical baby."

"Oh my father. I love when you concede. How much it turns me on. Suasive, as you put it. Look at me: swaying."


A camera, two people, four hands, the mirrors. How complex can it be? Nonetheless, some of the photos are unreadable. What body parts, how many bodies, whose, from which direction. Though she loves the more abstract images, the visually elusive, these are . . . incomprehensible. As if to remind them how arbitrary—how miraculous—seeing is.

The photos, when readable, lead them on, instigate. Also vary, depending on how one looks at, orders, arranges them. Chronologically, for instance. Or by category. Of, say, him in her mouth. Of her hiding in the blankets.

One day, the writer takes the photos to the Xerox shop, puts four or six shots per page. Collages. Does them in black and white. When she comes over, he shows her these new sets of images.

"Something I especially like," she tells him, "is how these become less precise now. More universal. Also catch recurrence, both of taking the photos and of making love." She smiles. "Time. And, my love, motion."

Love, motion. The writer thinks of a day they were

looking at the Polaroids. He was amazed, again, by shaft, labia, breast, nipple, tongue. What he'd seen, but not with this capacity to consider, assimilate.

His daughter said, "I'm compelled by this shot's composition, and the color."

"Composition? Color?"

"You know. Curves, straight lines, volumes, triangle of elbow, arm, torso. All the proportions. The deep cobalt of the bedspread."

Eye of the beholder, the writer thought, leaning over to kiss her. Woods; trees.

Please bring your camera when you come over next time."

"I will. I also just bought some film for the Polaroid. On sale."

"Thrifty baby. We must have two hundred Polaroids now."

"Is that a question?"

"Yes."

"Why do we want more?"

The writer nods.

"Well, wouldn't you say we want to make sure it's not a dream?"

To make sure it's not a dream. Usually, picking the

Polaroids up off the floor after they make love, they look through the stack. Some shots she wants to censor—her word—but always asks if he minds.

"No," he invariably tells her. Watches as she cuts up one image, another. What she eliminates are those in which she doesn't think she looks her best. That is, censoring has nothing to do with how X-rated, as she puts it, the image is. (Sometimes, however, though she wanted them taken, or took them, she won't look at the X-rated pictures, or, only days later.)

Sometimes, also, she jokes about how one day they'll have a museum show. She'll be curator. And, because she likes the more abstract photos, suggests MoMA in New York City will be the venue.

More than once he wonders why she agreed to the Polaroids in the first place, or why she was, is, not afraid of him having them.

"I trust you," she says several times, perhaps as a kind of wish. Or perhaps she simply wants anything that promises to serve her passion, curiosity.

One day he again asks why she consented.

"I didn't consent. You did."

"Sorry. I forgot who's in charge."

"Forgiven. As for your question, my father, I'd say it was initially like any photography. Catch a moment, frame narrative. Also, it could articulate the sexual between us. So much that was powerful required an outsider's view. Then, too, I wanted to see what you saw. Yes?"

"Yes."

"Beyond that, you and I are moved by the visual: the delicious shock of witnessing love as it takes such form."

" 'Delicious shock.' I like that."

"Thank you, my father. Finally, the photos have been a sharing, beyond the voyeurism and aggression, or objectification."

He thinks it over. "Pretty well argued, dear one."

"But."

He laughs. "But, my daughter, aren't we taking the photos to be proof, someday, of what was?"

She's silent, as if he's said they'll soon stop seeing each other. Not what he meant. His point, rather, was about the thermodynamics of photographs. They seem only to gain force with time, like that nude of a nineteenth-century woman the writer still admires. Her beauty piquant because, long since, it no longer exists. Not that the love between him and his daughter need end this week or this year, but that, one day, it surely will.

## YOU SHOULD SEE

She phones. Thesis almost done, prestigious university press about to send a contract.

"Hardworking baby."

"Like my father. You showed me how."

"I don't think so."

"I've taken so much from you. How focused you are. I'm learning to be like you."

"Thank you, even if it isn't true. Even if you shouldn't be like me. But anyway, your first book, my daughter. Just wonderful."

"It's not my first book. I'm already published."

"And how is that?"

"Your man John Donne: 'Love's mysteries in souls do grow, / But yet the body is his book.'"

Book of the body. Play of words.

"Was I all over my father last night?"

"No, baby."

"Guess what I'm doing."

"What."

"I'm ready for bed. I just dropped my panties. Now I'm getting under the covers. Oh, what a surprise."

"What."

"How wet I am. Guess where my hands are now."

"Can't."

"My fingers are molesting me. You should see."

Later, she tells him, "I don't think we could ever intentionally let each other go. How would you be able to do it?"

Her husband's been away; now they're about to leave on vacation. She's never loved anyone the way she loves the writer, she tells him, but being with her husband is essential to her sense of self, to her survival, even if her love of the writer supersedes that life.

Etc., etc., the writer thinks.

"How would you ever be able to let me go?" she asks again.

"How?"

"Yes."

"Well, say, if you travel with another man."

"That's a good one," she says, laughing appreciatively.

. . .

She comes over to the cottage for less than two hours, calls later.

"My Zeus. Did I kidnap you today for a change? You don't think this is sexual obsession?"

"I don't know, baby."

"You had me first, didn't you."

"First when?"

"In my whole life."

"How? When?"

"I was twelve. In the castle. You kidnapped me. I was crying. You tied me down. I was weeping, saying no, no. Then you started to come in me. I was so afraid, you were too big. But you did it anyway. You hurt me, you terrible man. You came and came and came. And then I came and came and came."

"Are you telling me your father kidnapped you, then violated you in a most brutal way?"

"Yes."

"So what happened? Did you call the police?"

"I was going to, but then you married me."

"Married you?"

"Yes."

"So I'm your father and your husband?"

"Yes." She pauses. "My love. Someone's coming. I have to go."

An hour later, she calls back. "Sorry, my love, where were we?"

"You were avoiding the truth. It was the word *someone*, as in, 'someone is coming.'"

"Sorry, my father."

"Yes." He gives it up. "I was saying I'm your father and your husband. I kidnapped you."

"Yes, my love. I became your slave during the kidnapping. I identified with you against the authorities trying to save me. You know, Stockholm syndrome."

"You mean, it's all just sexual for you."

"Yes. It's all your fault."

"I'm sure you're right. But why?"

"Well, it runs in the family, doesn't it?"

You're tired of this. You'll find someone else."

"True. Will you help?"

"You've been with so many women."

"Yes."

"You'll leave me."

"Yes."

"Just like that?"

"Yes."

"You won't worry about what happened to me?"

"No."

"You'll be with someone else?"

"Yes. Like you are now."

"It will take you, what, a week to move on?"

"You ignored my last point."

"Tell me. A week before you find someone new?"

"Dear one, I don't know. I had to pretend to nearly die to get you to even kiss me."

"Pretend?"

"You thought I almost died? You fell for that?"

"My Zeus."

"If I am Zeus, I'm not acting like myself. I'm behaving like some kind of granola god. I should be destroying your life. Phone call. Letter. You know, fuck things up. *Ka-boom!*"

"Please do. Then it will be out of my hands. But don't tell me you're going to. And forget I asked. And who knows what will happen. Probably nothing will change. I'll just spend years repairing the marriage."

"You see how tough it is being a god. Somewhere between total authority and none at all. When you think about it, what's in it for Zeus?"

"My Zeus." And then, as if suddenly aware, "Has anyone ever called you Zeus before?"

"All the time. 'Zeus, Zeus.' So tiresome."

"I created a monster, didn't I?" And, pensively, "Of course from the human p.o.v. the gods are always monstrous."

. . .

She hates to end phone calls, even when he's worn out by another marathon session. Though she's aware he's no night owl.

"Good-bye, my daughter."

"My love."

"Say good-bye."

"My love. There's no good-bye possible between us."

Difficult baby reluctant to be put down for the night, exhausted father ready for bed. Overtired, he uses her proper name, which long since seems reserved for moments of irritation. Which makes her protest, implore. She wants to be, insists that she is, his daughter. Only child.

EMISSARIES OF NECESSITY

Don Juans. His baby Casanovita. He skims a biography of Lord Byron. Bisexual masochist, pedophile, cross-dresser. Slept with his half sister. Showed one lover's letters to another. Byron: no role model. Still, the writer thinks of the boundaries he and his daughter have crossed. How many yeses.

"Don't ever do that again," she says, licking his finger-tips.

"Just leave my toes alone," he replies. Knowing how much they both enjoy non sequitur.

Non sequitur. Confused, the writer wonders whether they're already in the past. Is his daughter not only story, but story from then, not now?

157

He remembers a young woman he spent two nights with in his early twenties. It was during one of his many returns to Boston. Sonya was a painter, married to a jazz singer. They met because of a remarkable older woman, Leila, who had a gift the writer could then only begin to appreciate. In her early forties, a successful executive in Boston, Leila's chosen mission was to throw parties. Each a separate universe in which status and income counted for little. Music, dance, food—pleasures of the moment—were everything. A kind of carnival.

Once a year, Leila gave a party that went on for three days. That first evening, Leila introduced the writer to Sonya. "You two are made for each other." Joined their hands. As if ordained, the writer and Sonya spent the weekend together. Ate, drank, slept, made love. Never left Leila's house. On Sunday morning, Sonya woke him with kisses. "I have to meet my parents at church," she said, laughing, as the writer went back to sleep.

That was it. Sonya returned home to her marriage. A year later, shortly before the annual party, Leila was killed in a car wreck. Snow, ice.

The writer cherished his nights with Sonya, though without later wishing she'd been able to stay. They had what they had. He does now wish, however, that Leila were here. To talk to about his daughter. To meet her.

Then it comes to him: if his daughter could meet Leila, she could meet his mother.

. . .

Writer—dozing, waking. Ruminating. In college, he enrolled in a seminar on group behavior. His class was itself one of the groups being studied. High-tech social science: two-way mirrors, graphs, variables, video. One predicted behavior was that males would compete, with the male teacher and each other, for available females. In this group, there was only one woman. It finally dawned on the writer that he should ask her out. After class.

Half-asleep, and alone, the writer dreams he's telling this story to his daughter.

"So you two went out?"

"Yes."

"You made love?"

"No one in the group knew."

"What happened to you two?"

"The semester finished. I met someone I really liked. I don't remember our separation as at all tragic. We were coconspirators. The secrecy was compelling."

"Like ours?"

"Sort of, I guess."

"What else about her?"

"She was a redhead. Red pubic hair—brilliant red-orange."

The writer, half-awake, suddenly is unsure if he's

already told this story to his daughter; her response seems to echo something said, heard.

"I'm going to get my own redheads."

His rejoinder also seems to the writer something that already happened. "But, dear one, you're married."

Two in the morning. Not sleeping well. The writer makes himself wake up, asks himself how he can find out whether or not he already told her. Thinks he recalls one of the reasons he settled down the last time, for what turned out to be not forever but nearly ten years. That, beyond affection, respect, and trust, he'd tired of his own tricks and turns. So many different narratives. Had, finally, had enough of being unable to remember to which lover he'd told what.

To know his daughter has been to be without her most of the time, to separate or confront an ending over and again. And what kind of ending? Of what duration? How did I get myself into this? he wonders. So many impossibilities, threats, losses.

One evening, they see a video of *Black Orpheus* (1959). Set in the favelas of Rio during Carnival, this version of the myth has Orpheo as tram conductor and dancer, Eurydice a country girl fleeing the man trying to kill her.

The film is new to his daughter, and as if new to the

writer, so many years has it been since he first saw it, first heard its extraordinary melodies. How young Orpheo and Eurydice are, he thinks. And, how could he have forgotten how scarily quick Death is—in mask and skintight skeleton costume stalking Eurydice? Lithe, relentless, inescapable. At the end of the film, Orpheo, grieving, recovers Eurydice's body, carries her in his arms, her long hair flowing down, Orpheo himself soon to fall to his death.

Pensive, they lie on the bed while the video rewinds.

"I don't want to go back to that life," she says.

"But you will, or so you keep saying. That's who you are, it seems. There's love there, affection. Commitment."

She pulls herself up, looks down at him. "Am I Eurydice?"

"No, baby. Eurydice dies."

An easy no, but in a dream later that night, after she's gone, the writer carries his daughter in his arms, her long hair flowing down. Is she dead? Is he soon to join her? Or is it simply that what they've been together is going to die?

She never dreams, she tells him, but over a few days remembers several intense dream fragments. One is about hidden rooms in the writer's cottage—other women in the writer's life, secret, displacing. There's also a dream episode in which her husband is killed in a train wreck. Wish fulfillment? If so, only because it would make things easier. Still she's never spoken a negative word about her husband. And, finally, she summons up a dream moment in which the writer's in an ambulance. She's unable to convince the driver to open the door.

Then, a week later, two extended dream narratives.

*#1.* "We were in the park. You sat on a rock. I knelt down and unbuttoned you. People were there, but it was dark, and you said, 'Please.' I took you in my mouth. People did see us, and it got me nervous; they were people from work. Then I was with my husband on top of a hill, by a lake, and he jumped in to show how brave he is. I was very anxious, but he did come up."

"He came up. But did I come in the dream?"

"Terrible man."

"Did you put down a blanket on the rock for me?"

"Did I come, just by licking you? It was very erotic. I want to unbutton you now."

*#2:* "My aunt and I are at a play, front row. You're onstage, shirtless, holding some pictures. You're great, it's a love story. I can tell they're our Polaroids. I get uneasy because my aunt will see. I have to distract her. Meanwhile, you start making faces at me, to get me to laugh."

Some days later, she has a third dream. She's sitting on the front steps of the cottage, sees the writer coming back with a woman.

"Then what happened?" the writer asks, bracing himself.

"You said, 'Hi, baby, she's here for us.'"

"And?"

"I remember the vulvas touching. Kissing. Then you were in her mouth; I was watching, I wanted to see. I was saying, 'Please take me.'"

"To whom?"

"To you. I wanted you in me."

She tells him this from a pay phone. They haven't seen each other for nearly a month.

More twice-told tales. About: play she saw, colleague's e-mail. She's telling many things twice. Writer, storyteller, human—he can hear it.

"You're handling me," he tells her. "Stop it. Not a role I care for."

His mother's *froideur* in that photo of her at seventy, her bemused sense of life's many poses. Roles, parts the writer's played. A woman, recently divorced, he saw only when he wanted, and then just for several hours at a time. Always, her place. Passion, immediately, as soon as he arrived. Right then and there, except for the endless moment it took her to untie his laces, unbuckle his belt. Later, a shower, the two towels she'd put out. Conversation about books; she was a reader, beginning to write. Then the meal she'd prepared. Not what she wanted, she kept saying. No. But also, yes. A purity in such stylized focus. And collaborative: of course her complicity was required.

Parts played. Actress the writer once dated. Successful, a gypsy, always leaving for another location, tour. Wistful for domestic rhythms not lived. More than once, thud of script on front porch as they made love, UPS truck pulling away. Writer watching, again, as she'd grab a robe, run to see what it was.

One weekend, just after the writer came over, the actress told him she had to go to dinner with her agent and a producer. Business. Did he mind not being invited? She must have felt he acquiesced too readily: that book he was waiting to read. After a bath and putting on her makeup, she did a pirouette in the hallway, white skirt swirling. "Oh," she called to the writer, "I forgot my panties." Blowing him a kiss, pulling the door shut behind her.

His daughter: flirting with her fish, though an older woman friend warns that admirers may not be able to distinguish between flirting and seduction.

"My father," she says, "it's not a problem. I can only make love to people I love. Young men are too raw. It would be self-destructive to be with them. And anyway, how could I be with someone else if I'm with you?"

"Just what I've been wondering."

"But if you and I separate I'll be angry at my husband, and mourning."

"Again ignoring my point? All right. . . . If you and I separate, you'll have to be with the fish."

"Yes," she says. "But I won't want to be."

Also, more than once, she seems to be waiting for him to ask about her sexual life when they're apart. Past sexual life, if she's to be believed: she tells him she and her husband have not made love for months. She's been using medical excuses. Trying to be faithful to the writer, at least for this moment.

"Baby liar. Should I believe you?"

"Do you?"

"I think I do. It's your kind of gesture. And we're getting closer all the time, aren't we? Hard to deceive ourselves about that."

Later, she inquires about the woman who took care of the writer the night his father died. What the woman "really did."

"You mean, in bed?"

"Yes, my love. Please."

When he's done, she says, "Was it like this?" Pulls him close.

In the morning, he asks, "Who did you identify with in that story?"

"With you, my love. With her a little. I really identify with the act."

"What does that mean?"

"Now I don't feel excluded. I'm not jealous because you're telling me."

"And because it's a long time ago. And she and I weren't in love."

"Yes. But I think we should do it with everyone you've been with."

"And you'll leave me when I've run out of stories?"

"You could start again at the beginning. Tell the stories differently. Or better!"

"Or maybe I'll have to get new material. I'd be doing it for you."

"No, my father. Never. I'm yours. You're mine."

Photos: black-and-white of the author as three-year-old, pulling away from his mother. Love, dependence. Ambiguous, costly. Satisfaction that only and forever created new need. Anxiety about such need. Anger in response to such anxiety.

That wedding picture the writer searched for, couldn't find. Tore his desk apart for. Was it perhaps never given? Did his daughter bring it over one afternoon, show him? Was it that first time at the bay? And, what was it he so wanted to see again? What is it he's now not sure he's willing to guarantee, to persuade—inveigle—her into losing?

As so often, arguing with her though she's not there. Recalling their disagreement about the Tolstoy biography. What the writer didn't say, that at least part of him yearned to give her whatever she asked for. Story as confession, surrender, gift. About, for instance, what it cost to separate from someone you loved: no wonder his daughter's been unable to bring herself to do it. Or, price of a capacity to lose something simply to gain experience; the sense one could easily have been more loyal to someone so true. Diminishings; hearts rended. The growing understanding that he had from the beginning reserved the right to leave.

And, if his daughter wanted more, an accounting of what was never offered—for instance, those many children she was sure he'd had. Lives precluded—or, more than once, terminated—so that . . . so that, as it turns out, his daughter could be his only child. Fate, no doubt, all of it.

# ONLY OBLIVION

She has said to the writer:

"Let's make love, my love, for as long as we live. You're my dream, source of the most exquisite pleasures, the deepest joy."

"I want you to punish me for not being there."

"I could never leave that life. He'd never let me go."

"It would be false to deny us. I belong to you. We're meant to be."

"I'm not safe with you."

"You still don't think we're star-cross'd?"

Star-cross'd. The writer shakes his head. More *Romeo and Juliet*!

And her questions, her questions:

"What's the worst you could do to me?"

(Destroy her marriage, then leave her.)

"Have you ever been cruel?"

(Was the snake in Eden cruel?)

"How do you end a love?"

(Which love? he asks, but she won't say.)

And her escape scenarios:

"You could drive us off a cliff, but you'd never do that, would you?"

(Death solves all.)

"Knock me up."

(Unimpeachable excuse.)

He admires his daughter's effort at such narratives, as if their imperatives can solve her—their—problem. Stories: over the years, how the writer deferred, exorcised, or compounded so many problems.

"We can meet again in the next life," she says.

"You've probably already promised yourself in the next life."

"Don't worry, I'll take care of it." Meaning, she has, but she'll renege.

The next life. He tries to imagine how it would—will?—go. There they are, souls spinning through space. Waiting for reincarnation in an ether of Pure Lieder, longing, yearning. Being conceived, finally, then infancy—that near drowning in the wading pool yet another time; childhood (piano lessons? snow, sleet, galoshes?). Adolescence interminable. Driving lessons. Various lovers, blind need, the thwarted heart, wounds inflicted, all the years and years, until, finally, she's seventeen and he's forty-two, or she's nine and he's thirty-six, depending on which version of their first meeting and his abduction/seduction one goes by. Which version one believes. Relives.

New scenario. She'll stay with the writer thirty years, but call home every night. Simply what they're doing now, but more so.

"Cute. But you'll never be able to tell him. You're stuck in parallel lives. Living by tunnel vision. I should just do it for you."

"How?"

"Phone your husband. Tell him the truth. It will be a gift in some ways. You should be taking care of this yourself."

"My love. Do what you have to do. Maybe it's the right thing. We deserve to be out in the open. But then I don't think we'd ever be able to see each other again."

The writer ignores this. "Or maybe I won't phone."

"Then what?"

"I could send one of the Polaroids."

"No. Promise you won't do that."

"Why? Because someone else will hate you after seeing them?"

"That's true. But my love, my Zeus: the point is, the

Polaroids are for us. They're what had been unseen; what altered our vision; what our eyes desired."

Nagging questions: writer again asking if she can imagine leaving her husband, and again she says she can't even begin to. Could never hurt her husband in that way. Tired of himself, the writer thinks of Lear grilling his daughters, soliciting a love they shouldn't offer.

Once, his daughter is talking about her childhood in the castle. "My father taught me to read." The words hang in the air; she looks at the writer, stricken. "I meant, my mother's husband. I'm sorry."

After a long silence, she brightens. "See? Sometimes I do apologize."

The word *gossamer* comes to him. This story they created. So powerful, yet so easily subverted. And, he realizes, how exposed they'll both be without it.

Days without hearing from her, then a call.

"I've been seeing you everywhere," she begins.

"Except in person."

Strange, he thinks. As if she's trying to argue him out of understanding the meaning of what she's saying. Despite the extraordinary gift of renewing his love of story, she has him hearing all that's not stated.

"I'll be there soon," she says, "you'll just happen to me."

"Still want to be my daughter?"

"Please. I'll always be your daughter."

"I don't know. Time for hard choices."

"Can't."

Can't. What the writer planned to tell her. "Sorry, dear one. If you want to be my daughter, you're going to have to grow up." But he doesn't. Can't.


She hates feeling in jeopardy, afraid of going crazy. Sees the writer all the time, but no slipups. Or, not yet. Everything still in place: thesis, teaching, husband, aunt. Baby outlaw, but prudent. Afraid, too, of losing her only chance "to give it all up for love," but she won't do it, the writer's sure. Or, staying in her marriage, maybe she already has. Rilke's "you must change your life." Why pay such a price? Poor wet rabbit. Baby triumphant, baby uneasy.

"I'll make it up to you," she tells the writer as she leaves, but he remembers the phrase: just what she told husband one day when, her husband thought, she was again heading to her aunt's. Visiting her aunt so often, abandoning him, as her husband put it.

Early on, the writer promised to help her end what's between them if it was too much for her, and later, as her father, offered again. Now, he thinks, he should do what she can't do. Torn? Conflicted? Really, she is.

His daughter-the-reader. Virgil's *Aeneid*, one of her gifts to the writer. Aeneas, exiled after the fall of Troy, suffers countless perils on his way to the founding of Rome. Arriving in Carthage, he meets Dido, the widowed queen. Soon Dido is a victim of love. "Soft fire consumes the marrow bones. . . . Unhappy Dido burns, and wanders, burning, / . . . the way a deer / With a hunter's careless arrow in her flank / Ranges the uplands, with the shaft still clinging . . ." Inevitably, Aeneas departs to fulfill his destiny. And Dido falls on her sword, "foam of blood on the blade."

Baby Dido hates jeopardy, but cannot help herself. Or so she fears.

"Dear one," the writer asks, "do you think a father could be a Dido?"

Seduction. Stories he told his daughter those weeks they first met. And of course, years before that, seducer himself seduced by story. Impelled by what he read to become a writer, right when friends were, abruptly, no longer would-be artists but fledgling doctors, lawyers, academics.

And now? The writer's rereading Chekhov's "Lady with Lapdog." At the end, the adulterous lovers are in a hotel room, together but with an unknown future before them. Another gift from his daughter, Chekhov's tale, her belief in the recuperative power of art. Not that he wouldn't like to concur without reservation.

For so long, the writer's need of story was blind urge, incessant practice. Not surprisingly, then, he remembers when stories changed. It was toward the end of his mother's long stay in the hospital. Another moment that comes back to him often, something he tells, retells. That haunts. Which is that one day the writer read his mother several of her own poems, from a literary journal just arrived in the mail.

"What do you think of them, Mother?"

Propped up in the hospital bed, one eye covered with a patch, she stared into middle distance. "My poems aren't helping me here."

My father, could your mother ever have had two lives, like me now?"

"No."

"Are you positive?"

"How can I be? I was a kid then, and she's not around to ask."

"But you don't think so."

"No."

"My love, wasn't your mother passionate?"

"Not with me. With my father."

"Didn't you tell me I'm like her?"

"Yes."

"Well?"

"Possible, but I don't think so."

"I'm not as loyal as your mother was?"

"Please."

"All right. My father, tell me, was I virtuous when we met?"

"Yes, baby."

"Did I resist your advances?"

"Heroically."

"Didn't I say I just can't unlove someone?"

"That's what you said."

"Did I only give myself to you because you nearly died?"

"Your heart couldn't say no."

"I had to be true to what was between us, didn't I?"

"Yes. You had to."

"But being with my father makes me wicked. If we were together, I'd be virtuous again. That's who I really am. You believe that?"

"Yes, baby. That's the real story."

His lieder-loving daughter. The real story? He gives it a try.

Because of a desire to protect, or the burden of another's trust, its unspoken argument that one can choose not to change, or in compensatory self-sacrifice, with the erotics of penance on behalf of the infantilized spouse, who's to have no idea of the gift given . . . or because of the security of the familiar, solace of routine and social ties (not to mention a saga of preemptive separation so this father will never disappear as that father disappeared, and because Zeus can make it on his own, likes it better that way) . . .

In any of these narratives, the writer thinks, his daughter will be lost to him. Soon. Any moment now.

She phones long distance. "It's almost Father's Day," she says.

"So?" His parents never observed what they considered commercial holidays. "What about it?"

"No one could be a better father than you've been."

"Thank you, my daughter. And?"

"Well, what are you getting me for Father's Day?"

They laugh, and then it's time for her to go. Leaving him thinking. About their passion, her shrieking. Swell in from so very far away: becoming wave, cresting, breaking, exploding. Receding.

Years before, as usual studying the ocean at dawn, it occurred to the writer that death would come as a wave. Not that he would die in big surf, though he'd several times been scared to death. Pinned down, tumbling, turning, struggling for air—which way was the surface? Or, more frequently, standing on shore looking out, stomach beginning to churn as the surf rose, admitting to himself that he'd soon be paddling anyway. But this notion that came to him was different—death would manifest itself as a wave of energy in the form of light.

His heart. Amazing, that it keeps beating. Steady, undramatic. Over and over again. But, now, the occasional twinge getting one's full attention. Bringing to mind waves of energy in the form of light.

Writer, dozing, not quite half-awake. "Heartbreak," he mutters, as if it's the word itself that ended sleep, forced semiconsciousness. As if it's his relentless interest in language that brings him to this surface.

And then, slowly, in the dead of night, meaning intrudes, clarifies: "Oh, dear one, you're breaking my heart."

They're looking at the Polaroids together.

"You know, my daughter, as time passes they're gaining authority."

"How so?"

"Well, it's not just the accumulation of the acts portrayed, but the very existence of the photos. What's implied. The drive. All the extraordinary shared understandings to get to the pictures, to take them."

"They are beautiful."

"Clever baby. You know I'm trying to say something more. They've become an irrefutable argument."

"Which is?"

"When I look at the photos, I'm certain we'll never be able to give each other up. No matter what it costs."

His daughter's fervid imagination, and a corollary, squeamishness. "My father," she pleads, "don't say it that way. You're scaring me."

I love everything about you," she tells him. "You're the truest thing I know."

The writer, still going over it: perhaps with revision a solution will come clear, strategy that has worked with text for so many years. What if her problem is—merely— the moment of confrontation, that she believes she cannot give her husband an adequate story about separating. This hypothesis, the writer acknowledges, begs the question of what she's not able to tell herself about why she and the writer must be together.

"I don't think happiness is enough," she says, trying to articulate the hurdle she can't jump. "My happiness or yours or ours. It could only be a story of total desperation. Since we're together in this way now, I have no way of knowing that I can't give us up."

"Forget a story," the writer replies. "Show a Polaroid."

"I told you I won't stand for that."

"Don't worry, we'll protect the innocent. Nothing graphic. Man in black cotton robe, woman with head on his chest."

She's silent. There's a respite, but soon the writer is going at it again, even as he recoils from the sound of his own voice.

"You refuse to own up to the fact that your life changed. You can't go back to what you were any more than I can. The rest is sentimentality. But what's the point? Arguing never changed anybody's mind."

"No, my father, it's love, what you're doing. You're being faithful to us."

"I am?"

"Yes. But you have to let me go now, let me disappear, vanish, see if I return. Let me realize my destiny."

"Disappear? Vanish? Destiny?"

"Yes."

"But you want a trail of bread crumbs so you can find your way home. If you want to find your way home."

"Yes, my father. So there can be a happy ending."

Listen, dear one." Determined to act. Whatever the cost. His impetuous self redux—at last; his choler. Afraid of the ways he may fail her, of his anger at the threat of loss. Buffaloed by her withholdings, by indulging her, by his compassion for her.

"Listen," he says. "Once upon a time, there was a man, a writer, and, though he did not then know it, father of a baby girl."

"Yes."

"Whose daughter was married but who said she was his wife."

"Yes."

"She also said he was too sexual for her, although it could have been the other way around."

"Yes."

"So they decided to get married. Baby bigamist. Unfaithful to two husbands at the same time. Anyway, they married, despite obvious obstacles."

"How did they do it?"

"In bed. They exchanged vows. In that moment they were much changed. Gender oppositions overcome. Two as one, et cetera."

"Were they naked?"

"Yes."

"Like now?"

"Yes. And then they separated."

"Right away? Just like that?"

"Yes. This was a case of separation by marriage."

"But why? Who initiated the separation?"

"Both of them, without a word. The father knew his daughter was in a quandary. A predicament."

"I know what a quandary is."

"Sorry, dear one."

"Is it a-r-y?"

"Yes, a-r-y. So, this father, maybe for the first time—or so he told himself—decided to put aside self-interest."

"Was that the right thing for him to do?"

"Well, he felt his daughter was waiting for a miraculous reprieve."

"He wanted to work a miracle?"

"No. He was afraid something bad would happen."

"Like what?"

"Just something bad. But of course he couldn't believe what he was saying he'd be giving up."

"Which was?"

"You tell me, dear one. You know how the story goes."

Back in Honolulu, life apparently moving right on. Zen archer in Kapi'olani Park. Arrow drawn, held, released.

The writer alone, again, a *long* way away. Almost sure he's done the right thing. But oh, the doing. Those souls waiting for the next time around. Intergalactic winds howling. "Our misfortune," she'd said dreamily just before he left. As if it were beyond her control.

"I want you to be safe," she'd told him. Which put him in mind of his mother's struggle to hold on—for dear life—after his father's death. "Year of reversible loss," his mother termed it. As if there could be any such thing.

Mother. Daughter. At the beach: dawn, sun working up, over, and around Diamond Head. Ready to surf, the writer chats with an elderly woman who's there almost every morning. Tiny, ancient, all folds and wrinkles. As they stand in the shallows, she tells the writer that after her husband died she swam six times a day. "Six times a day," she repeats.

Just enough to stay afloat, the writer thinks, as he paddles out toward the reef. At the mouth of the channel, sitting up on the board to survey his domain, frigate birds wheeling far above, he has to choose: the break to the east, or the break to the west. Old Man's, or Suicides?

The writer laughs, wants to tell his daughter about the woman, about this moment of choice. "Poor baby ocean," he mutters.

Poor baby ocean? Poor self! Rising and falling with the swell, once again out on the face of the deep, he thinks of Henry James, who termed his loneliness the deepest thing about himself, deeper by far "than the deep countermining of art."

The writer's study. Locks she'd never noticed. One night, angered when, after they made love, she said she'd be going home in the morning, he slammed the study door, slid the bolt. Turning the knob, dismayed to be unable to come in, she started knocking. Kept pounding, crying, but he was determined she feel how it was to be closed out.

"What are we going to do with all the love between us?" she asked later, back in his arms. Baby passion, baby loss.

The study, his desk. That life-size model of the heart his doctor gave him. The writer often looks over at it, still marveling that one can peer into the chambers within, something his daughter liked to do.

His daughter. Her fastidiousness—"Have you washed your hands?" she'd ask, at the sink another time, faucets open wide. Purity and danger. Even as she'd leave the cottage there'd be an upwelling of hair. Single hairs, nests of hair, hair long enough to reach well below her waist. For days, weeks. As if replicating. Until she'd return again.

The writer does another walking meditation at dusk, savoring the almost-silhouettes of trees in full leaf. Such unstoppable exfoliation, beauty. His glass: half empty, half full. Nonattachment? How much is enough? One's self, but for how long? The writer laughs, thinking back to the feeding frenzy of models, those microuniverses, each as intricately alive as the gods made her.

His mind wanders, drifts. "What our eyes desired."

The writer has a shoe box of Polaroids, but what has he got? Those pictures of his daughter at the height of passion. In his possession, but what does the writer possess? Will Pygmalion's statue come to life when there's no more Venus? No Zeus.

Once, once his daughter asked the writer, "Which of us

took this picture?" Truly, no way to figure it out. Another time, she asked, "Still like me?" Naked except for deep blue panties with white stars. Purchased just for him, she says. "Do you?"

"Do I what?"

"Still like me."

"Yes, but it's complicated."

"Does my father still want me?"

"Yes."

"Is he disinheriting me?"

"Maybe."

"Disowning me?"

"Not telling."

"Please. Please . . ."

Baby gone away. Gone far, far away. He thinks of his daughter finishing yet another bath, standing in the tub, holding out the towel for him to dry her. Front, back, front again. Pointing to a place he missed, or didn't give enough attention.

"So," she said, "you still want me?"

"Yes."

And then she asked, "But wouldn't the pictures do just as well?"

# EPILOGUE

Dear one: here we are.
Book you said you wanted.
Book we've become.

# ACKNOWLEDGMENTS

My thanks to Sara Bershtel, associate publisher of Metropolitan Books; to my editor, Riva Hocherman; and to my agent, Jennifer Lyons of Writers House. I also owe much to the support of Gavan Daws, Ella Ellis, Fran Kaufman, Helen Lang, Laura Glen Louis, Stephen Rosenberg, Peter Santis, Terry Strauss, Anna Xiao Dong Sun, and Maria Tarkanov.